NO ORDINARY NURSE

NO ORDINARY NURSE

As an SRN who had two-thirds of a course in medicine behind her, Philippa James might be considered too highly qualified for the job as nurse/receptionist at a Health Centre. Dr Brent Charlesworth clearly thought she'd taken the soft option through lack of backbone – little did he know! Philippa was cer* nly not going to explain her reasons for wanting the job to this suspicious and patronizing do. en if he was also devastatingly attractive.

No Ordinary Nurse

by

Sarah Franklin

Dales Large Print Books
Long Preston, North Yorkshire,
BD23 4ND, England.

British Library Cataloguing in Publication Data.

Franklin, Sarah
    No ordinary nurse.

    A catalogue record of this book is
    available from the British Library

    ISBN   1-84262-286-2 pbk

First published in Great Britain in 1986 by Mills & Boon Ltd.

Cover illustration © Narborough by arrangement with
Allied Artists

The moral right of the author has been asserted

Published in Large Print 2004 by arrangement with
Sarah Franklin, care of Dorian Literary Agency

Dales Large Print is an imprint of Library Magna Books Ltd.

Printed and bound in Great Britain by
T.J. (International) Ltd., Cornwall, PL28 8RW

CHAPTER ONE

'So you opted out of your medical training, Miss James?' Doctor Brent Charlesworth tipped his chair back as he scrutinised Philippa. She felt like an insect on a microscope slide, but her head came up to look him full in the eyes as she replied:

'Yes. Circumstances obliged me to take a few months out. Unfortunately, those months developed into almost two years.'

'After which you felt unequal to picking up the threads,' he concluded. When Philippa remained silent he tipped his chair at an even sharper angle, his eyebrows arching cynically. 'But the fact remains that you are a State Registered Nurse. Don't you feel more drawn towards a hospital post? Life here at the health centre could be rather – shall we say routine, for a woman as ambitious as you quite clearly are.'

Philippa flushed at the implied sarcasm, wishing his chair would tip up as it threatened to do, depositing him on to the floor. He was quite undeniably attractive, she admitted grudgingly to herself as she regarded him – thick hair, the colour of ripe corn, and penetrating eyes of a deep blue-green. His deeply tanned skin spoke of a love of the open air – perhaps sport. But she was certainly not going to allow herself to be overawed by his good looks. So far she found him cold and suspicious. The other two doctors interviewing her for the post of nurse/ receptionist at Castlebridge Health Centre had been exceptionally kind and considerate in their questioning, but Doctor Charlesworth, the youngest of the three, seemed to be going out of his way to tie her in knots.

Stung, she lifted her chin, replying impulsively: 'Having been away from hospital life for so long I feel a little on the rusty side.' The moment she had said it she realised her mistake. She had played right into his hands. Even as the words left her lips she could see the light of triumph gleaming in the appraising eyes.

'I *see*.' His eyebrows arched even higher. 'And you were planning to rub some of that rust off on us, were you?'

Philippa's cheeks burned even warmer. 'Not at all! That isn't what I meant!'

He glanced at the notepad in front of him.

10

'Mmm – I see you've been caring for a relative for the past two years.'

'That's right.'

His eyes rose again to scrutinise her. They seemed to bore into her like laser beams. 'That was very unselfish of you. Not many young women would have given up a place in medical school in the middle of their course to do that. Was there no other way?'

Grey-haired Doctor Greg Frazer cleared his throat and leaned forward. 'I think Miss James has answered all our questions with great patience,' he intervened kindly. 'I don't think there's anything else we need to know at the moment.' He smiled benignly across the desk at Philippa. 'Thank you for attending the interview, Miss James, and for being so frank with us. We'll be in touch with you in a few days, when we've seen all the applicants.'

The middle-aged doctor rose courteously and accompanied her to the door. As he opened it for her he smiled. 'We shan't keep you waiting any longer than necessary,' he assured her. 'Good afternoon, Miss James.'

As Philippa passed through the waiting room she looked at the two candidates still waiting to be interviewed. Both were younger than she, only about twenty, possibly newly qualified SEN. As an SRN and with two-thirds of a course in medicine behind her, she wondered if she was too highly qualified for the job. Indeed, all three of the doctors had implied as much, though the two older ones had not been quite so blunt about it as Doctor Brent Charlesworth. She sighed with the irony of it as she went out into the September afternoon. Well, she was past caring, she told herself. If she didn't get this job she would just have to try for another. She wasn't at all sure that she could work with Doctor Charlesworth anyway. He had seemed so suspicious of her. She had encountered his type before, of course, during her time as a medical student. In spite of the fact that more and more women were taking up medicine nowadays there were still a lot of men in the profession who considered it a totally male domain and resented what they thought of as 'feminine intrusion'.

As she walked to the car park she remembered Doctor Charlesworth's analytical gaze and the patronising tone of voice he had used. Clearly he hadn't thought much of her. Obviously he was convinced that she had opted out of medicine and taken the soft option through lack of backbone. Little did he know!

Giving up her training to nurse her sister-in-law, Laura, through her illness and care for her four-year-old nephew had been the hardest thing she had ever done, and doing it had swallowed up both her career in medicine and almost two years of her youth! She could have explained all this at the interview, but she had made up her mind that coming to live in Castlebridge must be a new start for her and her small nephew. Simon had suffered enough in losing both his parents and she hoped to make a new life here for them both. Besides, she was damned if she was going to have anyone think she was appealing to their sympathy in order to get a job, especially Doctor Charlesworth. Not that *he* appeared to have any!

Philippa took out her keys and opened the door of her elderly Mini. Getting in, she sat for a moment, regarding the building she had just left. It was typical of so many health centres that had sprung up all over the country in the last few years; single-storied and built of red brick, it formed a sprawling 'H' shape and, as well as the surgeries of the three GPs, it contained a well equipped nurse's room, a dental surgery and various other rooms used as clinics for visiting therapists.

During the interview Doctor Frazer, the senior partner, had explained that they were working on a very tight budget. They had recently appointed a young social worker to deal with the many sociological problems arising from the large complex of housing estates that had sprung up over the past five years. Castlebridge, once a small country town, had been expanded to accommodate developing industry, which meant that its community was made up of overspill from the country's greater cities and consisted of people from very varied backgrounds. The elderly doctor had smiled at her.

'You can imagine, perhaps, some of the difficulties arising from that situation. This is why, for the moment anyway, we want to find someone who's capable of doubling the position of nurse and receptionist. Later on we hope to be able to increase our administrative staff.'

Having worked in the NHS before, Philippa could well imagine how tight things might be, and the necessity of putting the patients first. She admired the dedication of the doctors, and the prospect of working for them as nurse/receptionist appealed to her quite a lot. She sighed as she turned the ignition key and headed the car towards the car park exit. Beggars couldn't be choosers. It was unlikely she would get the job, and if she didn't there was nothing she could do about it. It was back to square one. She was almost down to the last of her savings and the need for a job was growing more vital as each day passed. She *must* find something and soon – even if it was scrubbing floors!

After becoming State Registered, Philippa had decided that she wanted to become a doctor. She had been in her third year as a medical student when tragedy had struck. Her brother and sister-in-law had been involved in a car accident that had killed her brother outright and left his wife paralysed. Their four-year-old son, Simon, who had been asleep on the back seat, was miraculously unhurt. After the initial shock the shattering truth soon became clear to Philippa. There were no other relatives. She had no choice but to postpone her career and go home to nurse her sister-in-law Laura and care for Simon. The unthinkable alternative was to let Laura become permanently hospitalised while her small son was taken into care. Not daring to stop and think about what she was sacrificing, Philippa had packed her bags and said good-bye to her fellow students and her training.

Caring for Simon and Laura hadn't been all hard work. In many ways it had been rewarding, and Philippa had been reasonably happy, doing all she could to help – until two months ago, when tragedy had struck again. A bad bout of 'flu hit Laura. It turned quickly to pneumonia and she failed to respond to antibiotics. Within a few days she had slipped quietly away, leaving Simon an orphan.

At first Philippa was numb. It had all happened so quickly. She had no idea what she should do. She had been appointed Simon's legal guardian, but there was very little money left of the small amount her brother had left. The child now went to school, but even so, it would be difficult for her to find a job that would fit in with his school hours. Losing both parents had made him a nervous, insecure child, and she knew she must do all she could to rebuild his world for him. That meant being there when he needed her.

The answer had come out of the blue – Philippa's first piece of good luck in over two years. She had been invited to a reunion at her old school, and there she had met Dorcas Mills, a friend with whom she had lost touch. They had talked for hours, exchanging news and their childhood friendship had bloomed again. Dorcas told her she was teaching in a primary school in Castlebridge. Since her marriage had broken up she had lived alone in her three-bedroomed house and rather than sell it she was looking for someone who would share it with her. As long as Philippa was looking for a change, why didn't she and Simon join her? Dorcas's working hours would mean that whatever job Philippa got there would always be someone at home to look after Simon. Philippa had leapt at the idea. It was a chance to get Simon away from all the old associations; to a totally new environment where he could start to live again as a small boy should.

Dorcas's house was in a small cul-de-sac on the edge of an estate about a mile from Castlebridge Health Centre. Philippa and her small nephew had been there for almost a month and already the little boy was beginning to lose the pale, haunted look he had worn since his mother's death. The country air had brought colour back into his cheeks and he had made friends with several of the local children. Each morning he went happily off to school with Dorcas, whom he had adored from the first. She had a no-nonsense approach with children to which he responded well, and Philippa felt confident that she had made the right move. As she put her Mini away in the garage she reflected that if only she could get a job things would be perfect – *if only*. It was proving to be more difficult than she had imagined.

As she let herself in at the back door she could hear Dorcas singing as she prepared the evening meal. She smiled to herself. At least someone was cheerful! As she opened the kitchen door the other girl stopped, looking round expectantly.

'Well, how did it go?' Dorcas was the same age as Philippa, but there all similarity between them ended. Whereas Philippa was small, dark and slim, the other girl was tall and statuesque. She wore her blonde hair in a short, boyish style and her favourite mode of dress, when she wasn't teaching, was dungarees or jeans, topped by workmanlike tee-shirts or sweaters. Outwardly, she was down-to-earth and outspoken, but Philippa knew that deep down there was a soft and intensely feminine centre that she allowed very few people to see.

With a sigh she threw her handbag and gloves on to the kitchen table. 'I don't think I have a chance,' she said despairingly, sinking on to a chair. 'They made it pretty clear that I'm A – too highly qualified and B – I've been out of things too long.'

Dorcas threw down the potato peeler and dried her hands. 'Oh, bad luck! Look, love, there *must* be something! What about the local hospital? After all, you are a qualified nurse.'

Philippa sighed. 'I might have to think about that, but I'm keeping it as a last resort. It'd mean working shifts, you see, and the chopping and changing would upset Simon. You know how insecure he still is.'

Dorcas nodded. 'What about the local factories? Maybe they're looking for industrial nurses.'

Again Philippa shook her head. 'For that you have to have your midwifery, and I didn't do that. I went on to my medical training instead.'

The other girl shook her head impatiently. 'That's ridiculous! As a medical student and an SRN you *must* know all about pregnancy and childbirth!'

'That's not enough,' Philippa told her. 'You need that little bit of paper.'

Dorcas's handsome face creased into a frown. 'Blast! Can't win, can you?' She brightened. 'Still, never say die. They didn't *tell* you you hadn't got the job, did they?'

'Not quite. But they might as well have,' said Philippa. 'It's a pity, it sounds so interesting. It's just what I wanted – except...'

Dorcas pounced. 'Ah, there's a snag!'

Philippa pulled a face. 'The youngest of the three partners.'

Dorcas's eyes narrowed. 'I know who you mean – Doctor Brent Charlesworth; tall, with corn-coloured hair. Rather dishy, don't you think – unmarried too.' She grinned. 'He's our "local boy makes good."'

Philippa pulled a face. 'That could account for his manner, I suppose. A big fish in a small pond! He might be dishy to *look* at – if you like that type,' she admitted grudgingly. 'But he grilled me unmercifully – asked me all sorts of questions that were totally irrelevant. He made it quite clear that he thought I'd abandoned my training because of inadequacy. He seemed determined to rub my nose in it too!'

'You shouldn't have let him get away with that!' Dorcas told her indignantly. 'Didn't you tell them about your tragedy?'

'No! You know I made up my mind when I decided to come to Castlebridge that I'd put all that behind us. It's for Simon's sake. Since Laura died he hasn't mentioned her or his father once. He's never going to adjust if he's for ever being reminded about the accident and the loss of his parents. You know how cruel children can sometimes be to each other.'

Dorcas nodded. 'I do indeed. But he's got to come to terms with it some day, love. If people don't know the facts, they tend to make some up for themselves.'

'I don't give a damn about that,' Philippa said stubbornly. 'The people who matter know the truth, and what the others say isn't important. I want to wait till Simon asks about Paul and Laura himself, then I'll know he's ready to start facing up to it and we can go from there.'

'But surely you'll have to tell the people who employ you,' said Dorcas. 'And you still haven't registered with a doctor. *He'll* obviously have to know.'

'I have,' Philippa told her. 'I registered this morning with old Doctor Martin. Everyone says he's a dear.'

Dorcas looked doubtful. 'Rather an *old* dear – he must be almost ready to retire! I'm surprised he took you on. What made you choose him?'

'Simon and I are both disgustingly healthy, so I hope we shan't need him much,'

Philippa explained. 'As for why I chose him, I suppose I was being optimistic. I thought it would be better not to be on the list of one of the doctors I worked for.' She smiled wryly. 'I needn't have bothered, though, need I?'

Dorcas was just about to make an encouraging remark when the back door opened and a small face looked round it.

'Dorcas, can Samantha come to tea?' The large dark eyes lit up when they spotted Philippa. 'Pippa! You're back. Are you going to work at the Health Centre?' Simon was tall for his six and a half years; slim and finely built like Philippa and with the same curling dark hair and expressive brown eyes. He crossed the kitchen to where she sat and stood in front of her, regarding her gravely. 'You don't look very pleased. Does that mean they didn't like you?' he asked perceptively.

Over the last two years the little boy had become finely tuned to the moods of others, and Philippa felt a pang of guilt. A six-year-old shouldn't be concerning himself with things like that. 'I don't know yet, darling,' she told him. 'I'll have to wait till they let me know.' She looked at Dorcas. 'Can Samantha stay to tea? Will the fish fingers stretch to another small helping?'

Dorcas smiled. 'Of course. Tell her to come in and wash her hands, Simon. I'm just going to put the chips on.'

Simon turned and ran out to fetch his companion, a little girl with red hair and freckles, who came shyly back with him.

Later that evening, when Simon was tucked up in bed and the two girls sat relaxing, Dorcas looked at Philippa thoughtfully.

'You know, you should get out more,' she said. 'Now that you're not so tied there's nothing to stop you.'

Philippa shrugged. 'After two years one gets out of the habit of socialising.'

'Then it's high time you got into it again!' the other girl told her. 'You wouldn't catch me getting into a rut. After Tom and I split up I was miserable for a while, but I soon came to terms with the fact that I wasn't getting any younger!'

Philippa laughed. 'As we're the same age I can only take that one way!'

Dorcas shook her head. 'Naturally! You know I don't believe in beating about the bush. You're only young once, and for some people it lasts for even fewer years than for others. Don't be one of those, Pippa. You'll regret it if you do.' She looked at her friend, her head to one side. 'What about that boyfriend of yours, the medical student you trained with? Why not get in touch with him again?'

'Peter?' Philippa lifted her shoulders. 'Not long after I left he wrote to say that he was getting engaged to the daughter of one of the consultants. I couldn't really blame him. After all, with us being a hundred miles apart and me unable to leave the house without a marathon of organisation it wasn't possible for us to see each other. Not exactly ideal circumstances for any romance to flourish in.'

'All the more reason for you to make a new start,' Dorcas said firmly. 'Now, I know you like music. There's a concert on at the Town Hall on Saturday evening, and I've got a ticket going spare. Why don't you go?'

Philippa's immediate reaction was to search for an excuse. Without even stopping to think whether the idea was attractive to her she said: 'Oh, I don't think so, Dorcas. There's Simon...'

'Rubbish! I can stay with Simon.'

'But it's your ticket. Don't you want to go?' Philippa asked.

Dorcas pulled a face. 'You know I don't go a bundle on that kind of music. You'd be doing me a favour. There's a group from school going. Let me tell them to pick you up, eh? You've met them before at the school Open Day you came to with Simon before the term started. They're a nice bunch.'

Philippa took one look at her friend's face and knew there was little point in arguing with her. As she got ready for bed that night she reflected that Dorcas was right. Not going out could become a habit that was hard to break. Just the thought of the coming concert and making the acquaintance of a group of strangers made her heart beat faster with apprehension. It *was* high time she eased herself out of her rut and back into circulation, especially if she was going to work among people again.

Dorcas was right about the group from school being good company. From the moment they picked Philippa up on Saturday evening they made her feel relaxed and at ease with their friendly chatter. There were three; a young married couple who both taught at the school and John Dixon, an older teacher whom Philippa had met briefly at the school open evening. Dorcas had told her that he was deputy headmaster and that he was widowed and aged forty-five. Philippa found him pleasant company.

During the course of the evening she learned that he lived alone in a flat quite close to the school and that music was his favourite relaxation.

During the interval they went to find coffee. The room set aside for refreshments was crowded and John found Philippa a seat and promised to bring coffee to her there. She was deep in thought and studying the programme when a voice spoke her name.

'Miss James, isn't it?'

Looking up, she was surprised to see Doctor Brent Charlesworth looking down at her. He looked very handsome, his golden colouring set off perfectly by a dark grey three-piece suit, and as she rose to her feet she registered, almost unconsciously, that the blue shirt he wore with it was almost exactly the same colour as his eyes. This evening the green seemed to have vanished from them. Perhaps, she speculated, it was because he was in a more relaxed mood. Suddenly she realised that she was staring at him and felt, to her intense annoyance, a warm rush of blood colouring her cheeks as she stumblingly said: 'Oh – good evening, Doctor.'

He looked her over, his cool eyes appreciating the slim figure in the grey suit, a froth of white lace at the throat; the dark hair that shone with rich chestnut lights, curling softly over her collar. His frankly appraising glance made her acutely selfconscious as he asked: 'Are you enjoying the concert?'

'Oh yes. It's ages since I went to one and it's a real treat for me.'

'I agree that it's a treat to hear one of the major orchestras here in Castlebridge,' he said. 'It's about the only thing I miss about London.' He sipped from his glass, looking at her over its rim. 'I take it you've had our letter,' he remarked casually.

Philippa shook her head, her heart giving a sudden leap. 'No – no, I haven't.'

'Oh? I'd have thought it would have reached you by now. Well, you'll get it on Monday, no doubt.' He glanced round. 'Are you here alone? If so...'

At that moment John appeared at Philippa's elbow, looking flushed and harassed. He was carrying two coffees.

'Sorry I've been so long,' he apologised. 'There was a terrible crush at the bar. I'm afraid some of the coffee has spilt in the saucers – oh!' He suddenly noticed that Philippa had company.

'John, this is Doctor Brent Charlesworth,' Philippa introduced them. 'Doctor, this is

27

John Dixon, deputy headmaster of Castle-bridge Primary School.'

Brent Charlesworth nodded briefly in John's direction. 'Good evening, Mr Dixon.' He looked at Philippa. 'We've met, actually. Well, I hope you enjoy the remainder of the concert, Miss James.' He turned, and she felt her heart sink. What was *in* the letter she hadn't received? She couldn't possibly agonise all over the weekend, wondering! Reaching out impulsively, she touched his sleeve as he began to move away.

'Oh, please – you said I should have had a letter...' She stopped as he turned to her, registering with a small shock how intensely blue his eyes were when he smiled, then she cringed with embarrassment when she realised how transparent her impulsive appeal had been. His smile was one of superior amusement.

'The letter? Oh yes, that's right. It was offering you the job, as it happens,' he told her calmly. He looked down into her flushed, confused face with slight surprise. 'I hope you're pleased. I *take* it that was what you wanted.'

Philippa forced herself to smile back. 'Thank you – it is.' Inwardly, she wondered if she was telling the truth.

CHAPTER TWO

On the morning of Philippa's first day in her new job she felt almost sick with nerves. Dorcas and Simon did their best to boost her confidence over breakfast, but it was no use. She couldn't eat a thing, and her stomach felt as though it was made of jelly.

As she helped Dorcas with the breakfast washing-up the other girl looked at her with exasperation. 'For heaven's sake! What are you getting yourself in such a state about?' she demanded. 'You know perfectly well that you'll be able to do the job standing on your head.'

Philippa sighed. 'It's just that I have the feeling that the decision to appoint me wasn't unanimous,' she confided. 'When I spoke to Doctor Charlesworth at the concert that evening I got the distinct impression that he hadn't been in favour of my appointment.'

Dorcas pulled a face. 'Well, who cares about him? You've got the job and that's all that really matters. You'll just have to show him that he was mistaken about you, won't you – take great pleasure in showing him how wrong he was.' She grinned impishly. 'It could be rather fun!'

Determined to be early on her first morning, Philippa was the first to leave the house, and Dorcas and Simon waved her off from the gate.

'They're lucky to get you, and don't you forget it!' Dorcas assured her. 'Just look what they're getting: an SRN *and* someone who's three parts doctor too!'

Philippa forced a laugh, wishing she could share her friend's confidence. As she drove to the surgery she thought about the brief conversation she had had with Doctor Charlesworth that evening at the concert. He didn't *have* to come up and speak to her – and at one point, when he had thought she was alone, she had been almost sure that he'd been about to ask her to join him. Yet there was still that cool reserve about him. She shook her head, remembering his direct, unsmiling look. The only time he had smiled was when she had impulsively asked what was in the letter – when he had the upper hand! Oh yes, she knew his type so well. As for what Dorcas had suggested, it wasn't worth the bother. His type made up their minds about people and never changed them. There was really only one word to describe him – bigoted!

She was parking her car in one of the spaces marked 'reserved' when she was hailed by Jenny Wishart, the practice secretary-cum-receptionist. They had met briefly at the interview and Philippa had taken to her on sight. She was a plump, cheerful-looking girl of about twenty-four with a halo of blonde curls and mischievous grey eyes.

'Good morning!' she waved as she walked across the car park towards Philippa. 'Welcome to Castlebridge Health Centre.' She hitched her shoulder-bag higher on to her shoulder and fell into step beside Philippa. 'I'm really glad it was you who got the job,' she confided. 'You were the only applicant who looked like my type!' She grinned. 'I hear you're an ex-medical student as well as an SRN. Very impressive!'

Philippa made no comment on the last remark. She was fast beginning to realise that her half-completed medical training could be a definite disadvantage. Jenny opened the door and held it for Philippa. From inside came the sound of a vacuum cleaner accompanied by loud, tuneless singing. Jenny gave her a wry smile.

'That's Gladys, our cleaning lady. She's quite a character. You'll be meeting her later. First I'll show you the office and explain the filing system to you. Then I'll show you the surgery and clinic rotas.' She looked at Philippa, her mouth pursed. 'It's a pretty hectic life here. I hope you've got a sense of humour – you'll need it!' She smiled. 'But I wouldn't work for anyone else. Our doctors are the best there are – all of them!'

In the reception office Jenny explained the layout of the building, then took off her coat and began to look out the record cards for the morning's appointments. 'We work on the appointment system here, thank goodness,' she told Philippa as she rejoined her in the office. She handed her a shiny new appointment book. 'This is yours. You'll be having your own appointments as practice nurse – you know the kind of thing – blood tests, dressings and so on. Oh, by the way, it's ante-natal clinic this afternoon. Doctor Charlesworth does most of the obstetric work and you're down to help him today.'

Philippa was taken aback. 'Oh! I thought the district midwife…'

Jenny shook her head. 'Poor Sister Taggart

is worked to death. She was really relieved to hear we were getting a nurse. Of course, she does all the house calls and delivers her patients at the GP Unit at Castlebridge District Hospital. It keeps her pretty busy, and she's got a case on at the moment. You'll only be filling in, of course. She'll be here whenever she can.'

'I see.' Philippa's heart sank. Right away she was going to be at a disadvantage with Doctor Charlesworth!

The rest of the morning passed in a mad whirl. Philippa had worked in a busy hospital, but morning surgery at Castlebridge Health Centre made it look like a rest cure! At half-past ten, when the last patient left Jenny looked at her with a rueful grin.

'Concentrated, isn't it? All that activity squeezed into an hour and a half! I think you did really well. You deserve a coffee. I'll put the kettle on. The doctors will be out in a moment for their appointment lists. They usually have a cup too before they set out.'

Philippa went off to tidy the nurse's room. Already she had had several dressings to attend to, three routine blood tests, a small boy with a foreign body lodged in his ear and stitches to remove from a minor operation site. In addition to that she had been called into Doctor Frazer's surgery twice to assist with female examinations. All in all it had been an eventful morning.

She arrived back at the office at the same time as a middle-aged woman carrying a tray of cups and a large pot of coffee. She had tightly permed blonde hair and wore dangling diamanté earrings and a print overall. Philippa sniffed appreciatively.

'Ah, that smells good!'

The woman put the tray down and regarded Philippa unsmilingly, her brightly lipsticked mouth pursed as she took in the neat blue dress covered by a crisp white apron and the small starched cap that topped Philippa's shining dark hair. 'How d'y'do,' she said with a sniff. She put the tray down on Jenny's desk and wiped one hand down the side of her overall before offering it to be shaken. 'I'm Gladys Moss – *Mrs* – I take care of the domestic arrangements here.'

Philippa shook the work-roughened hand and smiled into the shrewd, bright eyes that regarded her. 'How do you do, Mrs Moss. I'm Nurse Philippa James.'

Gladys' pencilled eyebrows rose. 'Not *Sister*, then? Just an ordinary nurse, eh?'

'I'm afraid so,' Philippa told her apologetically.

Jenny looked round. 'Nurse James is an SRN, Gladys, *and* she was training to be a doctor before she came to us,' she said. 'So she's no ordinary nurse.'

Philippa winced inwardly. She felt like 'something and nothing'. Why did her status always have to be explained to people? Clearly this piece of information left Gladys cold.

'Mmm, well – handsome is as handsome *does,* I always say,' she said meaningfully, and with this parting shot she turned and walked to the door. 'And if that coffee is cold by the time *they* condescend to drink it, don't blame me!' she warned sharply, one hand on the door handle. 'It was hot when it left that kitchen!'

As the door closed behind her Philippa looked at Jenny with dismay. 'Oh dear, I don't seem to have made much of a hit there!'

Jenny laughed. 'Oh, she liked you all right. That's just her way. You'd have *known* if she hadn't! By the way, Gladys is a single parent. She has a teenage son – Shane, as she'll no doubt tell you before long. Her husband did a disappearing act some years ago. She loves diagnosing the patients too if she gets half a chance, so don't say I didn't warn you!'

Male voices in the corridor outside heralded the arrival of the three doctors and Philippa busied herself in pouring the coffee. Doctor Frazer, the senior partner, smiled at her. 'Well, how has your first morning gone, Nurse James? I hope we haven't rushed you off your feet.'

Philippa smiled back into the kindly grey eyes. 'It's good to be back in harness again, thank you, Doctor.'

Doctor Copeland, a lean dark man with a brisk manner, nodded at her as he threw back his coffee almost at one gulp. 'Good to have you aboard, Nurse!' He looked at his watch. 'Well, better be off. I see my list of calls is full, as usual.' Folding the list in half and picking up his case, he hurried out of the office.

While Doctor Frazer discussed his morning's calls with Jenny, poring over the appointment book, Doctor Brent Charlesworth regarded Philippa over the rim of his coffee cup. 'I hope you enjoyed the concert the other night,' he remarked.

She nodded. 'Very much, thank you. And thank you for giving me the news I'd been waiting for,' she added. 'I shouldn't really have asked you. It might have placed you in

36

a difficult position.'

He shrugged. 'It might have been awkward if you hadn't been successful. As it was...'

She looked at him hesitantly. 'I – hope I shall be able to carry out the job to your satisfaction.'

He looked at her in surprise. 'I don't see why you shouldn't. You *are* a nurse, aren't you? That's what we advertised for.'

'Yes – but I...' Her mouth dried and suddenly she was biting her tongue in impatience. What was she thinking about – apologising for the inadequacy that was only in *his* mind? It was the one thing she had promised herself not to do!

He looked at her enquiringly. 'Yes – you were saying?'

Jenny saved the day, clearing her throat as she stood at his elbow. 'Sorry to interrupt, Doctor. Here's your list – not too bad this morning. By the way, I've asked Nurse James to help out at ante-natal with you this afternoon. Sister Taggart telephoned earlier. She's expecting to be at the hospital most of the afternoon with the patient she took in in the small hours.'

'Right.' He looked at Philippa. 'I take it you're familiar with ante-natal work?'

The implication was clear, and Philippa

saw yet another reason why he had been opposed to her appointment. As he was the partner who did most of the obstetric work in the practice one of his objections would have been that she did not hold her midwifery certificate. She drew herself up as tall as she could, determined to assert herself. 'At my hospital I worked regularly on the ante- and post-natal clinics,' she told him stiffly. 'I also did the usual spell on the maternity unit and, later, worked on gynae as a medical student.'

His eyebrows rose and the ghost of a smile quirked the corner of his mouth. 'Good heavens, Nurse! It looks as though you'll be able to teach *me* a thing or two with experience like that!' He took the list from Jenny, flashing her a brilliant smile as he did so, then turned without another word to Philippa and left.

When the two girls were alone in the office again, Philippa groaned and sank into a chair, her cheeks still burning from his cutting sarcasm. 'He *really* doesn't like me,' she complained. 'For some reason he's been prejudiced against me from the start.'

Jenny looked at her in surprise. 'Surely not! Why should he be? You're more than adequately qualified for the job.'

'That's just it,' Philippa told her. 'I get the impression that he thinks I'm trying to exploit the fact that I studied medicine. At the interview he hinted that I opted out because I couldn't cope, and he seems to be going out of his way to make me face my own inadequacies.' She sighed. 'I can't seem to put a foot right. Everything I say comes out wrong.'

Jenny shrugged. 'I wouldn't worry too much if I were you. I get the impression he's got some rather old-fashioned ideas about a woman's place – doesn't approve of them being clever. I think he prefers them to be fluffy and ultra-feminine. And if his girl-friend is anything to go by...' She stopped as the telephone rang.

Intrigued, Philippa waited until Jenny had replaced the receiver before asking: 'He has a girl-friend, then?'

Jenny noted the appointment she had just made in the book. 'What? Oh yes – Emma Francis. She's the daughter of a local solicitor and, between you and me, as clueless as they come.' She sighed. 'Still, with looks and cash like hers who needs brains? She's been away for most of the summer. Daddy treated her to a world cruise, would you believe? Because he thought she was looking a trifle peaky!'

Jenny sighed and cast her eyes ceilingwards. 'My dad just tells me to snap out of it when I try looking pale and interesting! Anyway, she's due back in a couple of weeks' time. Maybe that's what's making our Brent a bit scratchy – he's missing her loving arms!'

Philippa digested this piece of information. Doctor Brent Charlesworth's character was slowly beginning to emerge. 'I'd have thought he would have been married at his age,' she said, thinking aloud. 'He must be over thirty.'

'Thirty-five, to be precise,' Jenny tapped the filing cabinet beside her desk, her eyes twinkling. 'Consult Jenny Wishart, the Castlebridge oracle!' The smile suddenly left her face. 'Oh, I wouldn't want you to run away with the wrong impression. The information in here never passes my lips – at least not outside these four walls.'

'Of course not!' Philippa acknowledged gravely.

After lunch Philippa busied herself preparing the surgery for the ante-natal clinic. Jenny had laid all the patients' record cards neatly in order on Doctor Charlesworth's desk and she paused to glance through them.

'Everything all right, Nurse?'

She sprang back guiltily at the sound of

Doctor Charlesworth's voice. 'Oh – er – yes. I was trying to familiarise myself with the patients.' She felt her cheeks colouring again. Why was it that every time he spoke to her she felt guilty? It was something to do with his accusatory tone of voice and the cool, enigmatic stare of those blue eyes.

His eyebrows rose slightly. 'I like to try and take an interest in my patients as human beings. Too many people in our profession regard them as numbers on a card – statistics.'

'I assure you that I'm not one of those,' Philippa returned his unsmiling gaze. 'If I'd felt like that I would never have gone in for nursing in the first place. Personally, I've always considered that an interest in people has to be the first essential in any branch of medicine.'

For a moment he looked at her keenly, then he picked up the first of the cards on his desk. 'I'm glad we agree on that...' She had the feeling he had just stopped himself from adding: 'At least.' He picked up one of the cards from the pile on his desk. 'Tell me what you make of this patient, for instance.' He handed her the card. 'Mrs Hunter is in her late thirties and this is her third pregnancy. The other two aborted at three and a half and four months.'

'I'd say she was probably in a rather anxious state – and naturally so,' Philippa replied.

He nodded. 'Right. Unfortunately, it's a bit more than that; bordering on obsession. She's coming up to a crucial time now and I'm rather worried about her. Perhaps when we've seen her you'll give me your opinion – both as a nurse and as a woman.' He selected another card. 'Then, at the other end of the scale, there's Sandra – she's sixteen and unmarried – won't say who the baby's father is but is determined to have and keep the child.'

'What about her family?' asked Philippa.

'There's just the mother – divorced. She has to work to keep them both,' he told her. 'She finds it a struggle as it is. The poor woman's at her wits' end. She's still hoping Sandra will give up the baby for adoption when the time comes.'

There were others, and as he went through them, Philippa found herself becoming acutely interested. She forgot the hostile attitude of Doctor Charlesworth for a moment, learning a little more about him as he went through the list of patients. Although he was obviously very busy it was clear that he felt deeply for their problems. This was borne out later, during the clinic, when she saw him working with them; seeing a totally different side of Brent Charlesworth as he became absorbed in his work. The full charm of his personality was revealed as he joked gently with his patients, helping them to relax and coaxing information out of them almost without their realising it. Philippa found herself warming to this new side of him, especially in the case of Helen Hunter, a thin, nervous-looking woman in her fourth month of pregnancy. As Brent helped her down from the examination couch he smiled.

'Everything is coming along nicely this time, Mrs Hunter,' he told her reassuringly. 'As long as you take things easily over the next few weeks I see no reason why you shouldn't produce a perfectly healthy baby this time.'

Philippa helped the woman to dress while Brent went into his room to write her a prescription for vitamin tablets. Helen Hunter smiled wistfully at Philippa.

'He's very kind, but how can a man really know how it feels to lose a baby?' she asked. 'He does his best to reassure me, I know, but – well, he isn't even married, is he?'

Philippa smiled. 'That's true, but when we

have troubles no one else can really know how we feel,' she said. 'At least Doctor Charlesworth does try – does think of you as an individual and not just another patient.'

It was only as she turned that she saw him standing in the doorway and realised that he must have overheard her remark.

It was at the end of the clinic, as she was stripping the examination couch and checking the steriliser, that he asked suddenly: 'How long have you known John Dixon?'

Philippa looked up in surprise. 'I don't really know him at all. I took someone else's place that night at the concert and he was with the party.'

His face was expressionless as he sat at his desk writing up his notes. 'I see.'

Philippa knew she should leave it there, but although she tried she could not contain her curiosity. 'Why, do you know him?' she asked at last.

He hesitated. 'Not really – at least, only as a patient. He's a nice enough man. It's just that I was rather surprised, seeing you together. I wouldn't have thought you had much in common.'

Philippa felt a prickle of irritation. How did *he* know what kind of man she would find compatible? And what had it to do with him anyway?

Sensing her slight resentment, he went on: 'I know it has nothing to do with me, but perhaps I should warn you that John was very happily married.'

Philippa stared at him. 'Is that relevant? I don't quite see…'

He put down his pen and looked at her. 'All right. If you want me to spell it out for you – I get the impression that he'd like to be married again.' He shrugged. 'There's no need to look so affronted. It's just a friendly warning.'

'And one that's entirely unnecessary,' she told him hotly. 'If you're afraid I'll rush off and marry the first man who asks me – let you down, you needn't worry, Doctor, I have no plans to marry either now or in the foreseeable future.' She crossed to the wash basin and began to wash her hands vigorously. 'Perhaps you're wondering why I'm not already married or engaged!' She turned to look at him and was slightly gratified by the look of surprise on his face.

'Not at all. The question hadn't even occurred to me,' he told her. 'Obviously your chances of any kind of social life have been curtailed – nursing an invalid.' He cleared his throat. 'I meant only to warn you

45

that John is a rather serious man and...'

'Thank you!' she interrupted, furious at his patronising tone. 'I shall bear your warning in mind – if ever I meet him again! You're right about my social life,' she told him. 'It's been non-existent over the past couple of years, but that doesn't mean I'm ready to throw myself at the first man who looks twice at me!' Her heart was beating fast by now and the next remark slipped out in the heat of the moment, before she could stop it: 'It shouldn't surprise *you* to know that for some people there's more to life than marriage and homemaking. Obviously you have no desire for the state yourself!' She dried her hands and hung up the towel, paying meticulous attention to its folds, glad of the excuse to turn away and hide the warm flush that burned her cheeks.

There was a moment's silence before he said: 'Thank you for making your feelings so abundantly clear, Nurse. I'm quite well aware that patients like their GP to be married, but, like you, I'm not so dedicated that I'll commit myself to the first attractive face I see. Obviously neither of us has met anyone worthy of sharing our lives with, so it seems we do at least have that in common.' He stood up and began to get ready to leave, checking his case and snapping it shut. Philippa's heart-rate slowed and she began to regret her volatile reaction. She was searching her mind feverishly for some words to put it right without sounding like an apology when he turned to her from the door.

'Just one thing – please don't feel you have to make excuses for me to the patients again, eh?'

He closed the door firmly behind him and Philippa leaned limply against the desk. Just for a while during the clinic, she had seen that other side of him – the blue-eyed side, dedicated and charming – had thought that maybe the two of them could get along after all. But now... She visualised the sea-green flash of his eyes as he had delivered that parting shot, and winced.

Slowly she went to change out of her uniform. As she zipped up her skirt she was dismayed to discover that she was shaking. Why had she let his remarks about John Dixon get to her like that – allowed herself to fly off the handle? She must have sounded like a touchy, soured old maid! What made it worse was that she knew he was right. She *had* found John Dixon a rather intense, over-serious man, in fact it had crossed her mind that Dorcas just might be palming her off on him. It was quite clear by the way he had spoken that John was keen on Dorcas and, with her own marriage in ruins, she was definitely not looking for another serious relationship.

'Damn!' Philippa bit her lip as she walked out to the car park. She would have to let her touchiness go and spoil everything just when they'd begun to establish a reasonable working relationship. Now she owed him an apology, and *that* would put her right back where she had started!

CHAPTER THREE

The practice meeting at Castlebridge Health Centre coincided with the evening of the PTA dance. Dorcas was annoyed when Philippa told her over supper the night before.

'You're not trying to duck out, by any chance, are you, Pippa?' She looked at her friend, eyes narrowed suspiciously. 'You haven't been anywhere since that concert at the Town Hall and that was weeks ago. If I thought…'

'I promise you I'm not ducking out,' Philippa assured her. 'Apparently these practice meetings are very democratic affairs. Everyone gets to air their views. Doctor Frazer said he particularly wanted me to be there this time. Perhaps they're going to ask for my resignation,' she ended gloomily.

Dorcas threw up her hands in despair. 'There you go again! You know perfectly well that you're doing a good job, so why do you say that? Besides, didn't you tell me that the new social worker was arriving today? I dare say they want everyone there to meet him.'

Philippa nodded. 'Of course, that's true. I'm still not getting on too well with Brent Charlesworth, though. I did apologise for being touchy that first day, but it doesn't seem to have done much good. Since then he's hardly spoken to me.' She looked at Dorcas across the table, attempting to look more cheerful. 'Still, I don't suppose the meeting will last all that long. I'll slip home and change, afterwards, then come on.'

'Well, mind you do,' Dorcas said warningly. 'If you're not there by supper time I shall send a search party out for you.' She laughed. 'If they still had dance programmes like our grandmothers did I could have filled yours up for you in your absence!'

'Yes, and I can guess whose name would be beside every dance,' Philippa told her. 'Don't think I didn't catch on to your little game. You tried to palm John Dixon off on me, didn't you? The poor man's obviously besotted with you. He hardly talked of anything else that evening!'

Dorcas groaned. 'Don't!'

'What's the matter, don't you like him?' asked Philippa.

'I like him very much. The trouble is that

he obviously has his sights on a deeper relationship than mere friendship.' She sighed. 'It's a pity, he's very pleasant company. Life can be very complicated sometimes.'

Philippa smiled wryly. 'Well, that's something I know *all* about!'

'Just one thing...' Dorcas warned. 'Don't breathe a word about this in front of Simon. That child is so perceptive! He's already noticed that John pays quite a lot of attention to me and I don't want *him* getting ideas too. Before you know it the school grapevine will have us engaged!'

The term was five weeks old and Philippa was delighted at the way her small nephew had settled down at his new school. Of course, having Dorcas there had helped, even though she wasn't his teacher. They travelled in together each morning and although Simon sometimes walked home with his friend Samantha, Dorcas was always close at hand to keep an eye on him. His work seemed to be improving too.

'Have you heard him read lately?' Dorcas asked as they cleared the table together. Philippa shook her head. 'Why don't you go up before he settles down to sleep?' Dorcas suggested. 'I'll wash up. He brought his latest reader home with him this afternoon.

I know he's dying to show you how well he's doing.'

Upstairs in the pretty little bedroom at the back of the house Philippa found Simon looking at a large picture book and talking to himself as he often did. She put her head round the door.

'Hi there. Are you asleep?'

Simon quickly closed his eyes. 'Yes,' he said, trying not to giggle.

'Right, mustn't wake you, then.' The joke was a ritual between them. Simon played the next move, sitting up suddenly and shouting:

'I've woken up!'

Smiling, Philippa came in and sat on the edge of the bed. 'I'm glad, because Auntie Dorcas tells me you've brought your reading book home. I was hoping to hear you read it.'

Simon dived under his pillow and came up with the reader. He surprised Philippa by reading through it quite quickly from beginning to end.

'That's *very* good!' she said. 'Do you like your new school?'

He nodded. 'Most of it, yes.'

'And you like living here in Castlebridge?'

He was silent for a moment, staring at the cover of the reading book, then he looked up at her. 'Are we going to live here for ever, Pippa?'

She smoothed the tousled hair back from his forehead. 'Yes, I think so. You do like it here, don't you, Simon?'

He frowned. 'Yes. I like school and Auntie Dorcas and this house and – and Samantha.'

'Is there something you don't like?' Philippa probed gently. For a moment he looked wistful, then suddenly he smiled and threw his arms round her neck.

'No. I like it all – as long as you're here, Pippa.' He drew back a little to look into her eyes. 'You won't go away, will you?'

Philippa swallowed hard at the lump in her throat as she hugged the fragile little boy close. 'Of course I won't. We'll be together for always. I promise you.' She kissed him, then laid him gently back against the pillows, tucking in the covers firmly. 'Off you go to sleep now.'

'See you in the morning.' He snuggled down happily, his eyelids already heavy. Philippa stood up.

'See you in the morning. Night-night.' On the landing outside the closed door, she stood for a moment, her forehead creased in a frown. Deep down Simon was still suffering from the loss of his parents. It was odd that he had never spoken about them. When his father had died he had been too young to understand fully, but when Laura had died Philippa had done her best to explain her death to him. He had received her explanation with a calm acceptance that had left her at a loss. If only he had asked more questions she would have been sure that he understood. She sighed. All she could do was to try and make him feel as happy and secure as possible.

The practice meeting was held in the doctors' common room after evening surgery and Jenny had prepared the room earlier, setting the chairs out at the oblong table, a pencil and notepad in front of each place. 'Just like a board meeting,' Philippa thought to herself as they filed in. As they took their places she noticed that the seat opposite her was empty and soon realised that Doctor Brent Charlesworth, who had not been in surgery this evening, was absent. Doctor Frazer took his place at the head of the table and smiled round at everyone.

'I particularly wanted everyone to be here this evening because I'm not sure that everyone has had the chance to meet our new social worker, Nick Cornish. Unfortunately Doctor Charlesworth can't be with us as he was called out on a case earlier, but I'm hoping he may be able to look in before the meeting comes to a close.' He smiled at the young man at the far end of the table. 'I'm sure Nick will be a great asset to the practice.'

To Philippa, Nick Cornish looked almost impossibly young. A tall, gangling young man with a shock of red hair and an incipient beard, he looked hardly old enough to have left college, and she wondered just how experienced he was in the kind of problems he was here to sort out. He rose to his feet and smiled round at everyone.

'Thank you, Doctor, and hello, everyone. I'm sure we're all going to get along famously together,' he said enthusiastically. 'I know that if we don't it won't be my fault. I've had a good look round Castlebridge and I'm sure I'm going to find it a pleasant place to work in.'

As he sat down Sister Taggart, who was sitting next to Philippa, murmured under her breath: 'Hardly out of nappies, by the look of him! Talk about in at the deep end! I'd say he had one hell of a shock coming.'

The meeting followed its usual course, not much of which affected Philippa. She was just wondering why Doctor Frazer had been so insistent that she should attend the meeting when he got to his feet and cleared his throat.

'I suppose this comes under the heading of any other business,' he began. 'For some time past we have felt that there is a strong need for a counselling clinic here in Castlebridge, and I was wondering if we might initiate one here at the Health Centre. Now that we have a social worker on our staff I think it might be a good time to start thinking seriously about it.'

Once again Sister Taggart nudged Philippa. 'Does he think we're having too much spare time – or what?' she muttered ironically under her breath.

Doctor Frazer looked round the table. 'Does anyone have any suggestions to make – Nurse James?'

Philippa was taken aback. Reluctant to commit herself, she looked round the table at the other faces, wishing that she could have had notice of the question and that she knew the views of the rest of the staff. 'Well...' she said slowly. 'I'm not quite sure what use I'd be, but of course I'd be willing to help in any way I could.' She looked around at the others. 'Are we sure that the patients themselves want this?'

The elderly doctor smiled benignly at her. 'That's a good point. Perhaps we might have a public meeting to find out. Thank you, Nurse. As for wondering what help you could be, I assure you that everyone here has something to offer. Apart from our collective medical knowledge, we've all experienced life's trials and traumas and learned from them, haven't we?' A hesitant murmur of agreement went round the table and he went on: 'As I'm sure you all know, there is never enough time in the course of surgery hours to get to the bottom of patients' problems. Many of the trivial complaints they bring to us are simply the products of deeper, underlying problems, and this is where I feel we might help. If they felt there was help of a more personal nature at hand, especially from people they already know and trust, we might not find our conventional surgeries so crowded.'

Nurse Taggart broke in: 'Are you suggesting that we should set up in opposition to the Samaritans or the Marriage Guidance Council, Doctor?' she asked in the tone she reserved for her patients' recalcitrant husbands. Doctor Frazer shook his head.

'Oh no! That's just the point. I'm hoping

that we'll be able to keep things on a much more neighbourly basis – and probably prevent things getting to that stage.'

Nick Cornish jumped in enthusiastically. 'Well, *I* think it's a splendid idea.' He smiled eagerly, showing two rows of white, slightly crooked teeth and reminding Philippa of a friendly puppy.

Sister Taggart spoke again. 'May I ask just how much time we should be expected to give to this project, Doctor?' she asked tartly.

He shook his head. 'Just for the moment I'd like you all just to go away and think about the idea. Time enough at the next meeting to start planning the mechanics of it – that is if you're all agreeable.'

In the nurse's room as they prepared to leave, Sister Taggart looked at Philippa critically. 'Well, what did you think of that?'

Philippa frowned. 'I'm not sure. I'd like to do as Doctor Frazer said – go away and have a good think about it.'

'Well, it's up to you, of course,' the midwife said as she pulled on her coat. 'But personally I can see it taking up most of our free time. Anyone would think we hadn't enough to do already!'

Philippa nodded. 'That's obviously something we shall have to sort out at the next meeting.'

Sister Taggart opened the door and stood framed in the doorway as she delivered her parting shot. 'You missed a golden opportunity when he asked you what you thought. You should have *told* him straight and nipped the idea in the bud. Whoever thought this one up needs his head examining, if you ask me!'

Philippa stared at the open doorway, taken aback at the vehemence of the midwife's words. She had been taken off guard when Doctor Frazer picked on her. Besides, for all she knew, the others might have been wholeheartedly in favour of the plan. As she turned away a voice startled her.

'I take it Sister Taggart isn't keen on the counselling clinic idea?'

She spun round and came face to face with Brent Charlesworth. 'Oh! – I thought you were out on a call,' she muttered. 'How did you know…'

'I was in my surgery next door, writing up a report,' he explained. 'I'd have to be stone deaf not to have heard her.'

'But you weren't at the meeting,' Philippa went on superfluously.

He smiled bleakly. 'So how did I know

about the counselling clinic? Easy – because the idea was mine in the first place.'

'Oh!' Philippa was struck silent, acutely embarrassed as she tried to remember what she had said about the idea herself.

'Unfortunately I was called out, so I couldn't be at the meeting,' he went on. 'Otherwise I might have been able to set some people's minds at rest.'

Philippa stole a surreptitious look at the office clock, wondering how much time she would have to get ready for the PTA dance. Her preoccupation did not escape his notice.

'Do you have a date, Nurse James?' he asked sharply. 'I'm sorry if I'm keeping you from it.'

'Oh no,' she said quickly. 'It was just...' But she found herself talking to the empty doorway. A moment later the slam of the outer door told her that he had left the building.

By the time she got home Philippa had very little time left in which to get ready. Simon was staying with his friend Samantha for the night. Luckily he had seen it as a great adventure, and Philippa had been relieved. He had never been away from home before and she had been half afraid to suggest it.

The house was quiet. Dorcas had already left; being on the committee, she had had to be there at the start of the evening. Supper was to be served at nine-thirty. Philippa looked at her watch. It was almost nine now, she would have to hurry. She took a quick shower and re-did her make-up. As she opened the wardrobe she found herself grateful for the fact that there was little problem about what to wear. The life she had led over the past months hadn't included much socialising and the only dress she possessed that could be remotely described as festive was the one she had bought for the school reunion. She pulled it out now and slipped it over her head. It was made of deep blue chiffon, the skirt finely pleated and the bodice close-fitting and low at the neck. She surveyed herself in the mirror, her head on one side. Was it too dressy for a school supper dance? She shrugged. It was the only thing she had got, so it would just have to do. Besides, there was no time to change now.

When she arrived at the school the evening was in full swing. Everyone seemed to be in a party mood and she stood uncertainly in the doorway watching. Most people seemed to be circling the floor, dancing to the small group that had been hired for the evening. Philippa felt hopelessly out of place. Over the past months she seemed to have forgotten that these kind of occasions existed, and now she felt out of her depth. She knew a sudden moment of near-panic and was just turning to leave again when she felt a light touch on her arm.

'Not leaving again so soon, surely?' She turned and, to her amazement, found herself looking up into the questioning eyes of Brent Charlesworth. Her heart seemed to skip a beat as she mumbled:

'Oh – no – I just...'

His hand grasped hers firmly and he drew her towards the crowded dance floor. 'Might as well break the ice. What do you say?'

Before she had time to reply she found herself held in his arms, matching her steps to his. She looked up at him. 'I'd no idea you were coming here this evening,' she remarked.

He smiled. 'Of course you hadn't. Why should you? My aunt happens to be on the board of governors and I promised her I'd look in.' He looked down at her, one eyebrow raised. 'What happened, did your date stand you up?'

Philippa felt her cheeks colouring. 'I didn't have a date,' she told him. 'I'm here for much the same reason as you. The girl I share a house with is a teacher here.' Suddenly through a gap in the dancers she saw Dorcas, dancing with John Dixon. The other girl caught her eye and waved. 'That's her,' Philippa said. 'We were at school together.' She looked up into the face that was so close to hers and was suddenly acutely aware of his sheer maleness, the spicy scent of his aftershave, the strength emanating from him and the warmth of his hand through the thin material of her dress. She felt unaccountably disquieted by his nearness; the pressure of his thigh against hers as they danced. As they reached the corner of the room which had been roped off for refreshments he raised an eyebrow at her.

'Would you like a drink? I dare say you barely had time to change after the meeting – like me.'

She nodded. 'I'd love one.'

The corner had been set out with small tables and he led her to one of these. 'What will you have?' he asked.

She shrugged. 'I don't know – a glass of

white wine would be nice.'

As he put the drinks down on the table a few moments later he said: 'By the way, I was called out to Mrs Hunter, a threatened miscarriage.'

'Oh no! Is she all right?' Philippa looked up at him anxiously.

He shook his head. 'All in her mind, I'm glad to say. This is a bad time for her. She lost the others at this stage. I'm hoping that once we get her past the fourth month she'll be more relaxed.' He took a sip of his drink and looked at her. 'By the way, I'd like her to have an epidural for the birth. She's so tense that I feel her labour could be protracted. You seem to get along with her. How about having a chat to her next time she comes in?'

Philippa frowned. 'Isn't that Sister Taggart's province? I don't want to ruffle any feathers.'

Brent pulled a wry face. 'Tag's a good sort, but she is rather one of the old school.' He grinned. 'One of the "Mind your own business and let the midwife get on with it" kind.' He lifted his glass and looked at her over the rim. 'Just between ourselves, she isn't what you might call the soul of tact.'

Philippa laughed. 'Well, all right, if you really think I could help. I'll do what I can.'

She lowered her eyes, looking into her glass, aware that he was studying her face. At last he asked:

'How are you settling down here?'

She found herself colouring. This new, gentler approach was something she wasn't prepared for. 'Oh, fine, thank you.'

'You're liking the work – not finding it too routine?'

'Not at all.'

'And you don't regret...' What it was she was supposed to regret, she never found out, for at that moment a tall, well built lady advanced on them. She wore a black dress encrusted with sequins and her grey hair was blue-rinsed and set in firm waves and curls.

'Brent!' she cried triumphantly. 'So you *did* make it after all! My dear, I'm so glad.' She looked at Philippa enquiringly, her astute blue eyes appraising her. 'And who is this young lady? Aren't you going to introduce me?'

Brent stood up and kissed her on the cheek. 'I did try to catch your eye,' he told her, 'but you were busy bending the Headmaster's ear, as usual!' He turned to Philippa. 'This is Philippa James, our new nurse at the Health Centre. Philippa, this is my aunt, Miss Angela Stone.'

It was the first time he had actually used her Christian name and as she stood to shake the hand of the woman to whom she was being introduced, Philippa found herself wondering yet again at his change of mood. This evening he seemed quite a different person.

Miss Stone grasped Philippa's hand warmly in a firm grip. 'How nice to meet you, my dear.' She sat down in one of the vacant chairs at the table, settling herself comfortably. 'Now do tell me all about yourself. I always make it my business to get to know Brent's friends...' But she got no further. Philippa found herself firmly grasped round the waist and spun on to the dance floor again. Once they were out of earshot Brent looked down at her apologetically.

'Sorry about that. Aunt Angela is a dear, but she practically brought me up and she still thinks of me as ten years old. It can be extremely embarrassing!'

Philippa laughed. 'She seemed very nice – the little I saw of her.'

'Oh, make no mistake, she *is*,' he said firmly. 'One of the best. I owe everything to her.'

Looking up at him, Philippa saw from the

set of his mouth that the conversation was closed. Obviously he thought a great deal of his aunt and didn't want his words interpreted as criticism.

As they circled the floor Brent picked up the conversation they had been having before.

'Asking you to speak to Helen Hunter was precisely the kind of help I envisaged us being able to give at a counselling clinic,' he told her. 'You see, it isn't always the obvious person who is best qualified to help when it comes to the crunch. My idea would be to hold it once a month and to have one representative from each branch present: a nurse, a social worker, a doctor and so on, working on a rota. Of course, it would have to be done on a voluntary basis at first. The partners could refer patients to it at their own discretion.' He looked at her. 'What do you think?'

Philippa considered for a moment. 'It *sounds* all right – in theory. I suggested at the meeting that we might ask the patients what they think of the idea. After all, it is for their benefit and we could hardly do it without them.'

'That's a good idea!' He shook his head impatiently. 'What a pity I couldn't be at the meeting tonight. We might have arranged a date for that and got the ball rolling.'

The dance ended and supper was announced. Dorcas found Philippa and bore her off to the table she had reserved.

'Well! You seem to have forgotten your differences with the dashing Doctor Charlesworth tonight!' she remarked with a twinkle. 'Buried the hatchet, have you?' She laughed. 'If you're not careful I shall begin to think that all that aggro between the two of you was just a blind! You know what they say about the nearest thing to hate...'

Philippa restrained herself from making the reply that rose to her lips. Instead she said: 'If you must know, we were talking shop most of the time. Anyway, wasn't that John Dixon I saw you dancing with just now?'

Dorcas grinned goodnaturedly. 'Touché! No need to get ideas, though. I could hardly be rude to him when he asked me, now could I?'

They helped themselves from the buffet table and then returned to their table. Philippa nodded across the room to where Brent was sitting with his aunt. 'You never told me that Brent had an aunt on the board of governors.'

Dorcas cocked an eyebrow at her, pausing with a forkful of chicken halfway to her mouth. 'Ah – *Brent* now, is it? We *are* coming along!' When Philippa failed to rise to the bait she went on: 'Yes, I believe Miss Stone was his mother's sister and brought him up, more or less. His mother's a rather dynamic lady by all accounts – took over the family business when her husband died and became so absorbed in it that her family hardly ever saw her.'

'I see.' Philippa was aware that Dorcas was still talking – had moved on to something quite different now, but she was preoccupied with her own thoughts. So Brent's mother was a career woman, was she? Could that be his reason for disliking ambitious women? It might well be.

'…and it seems they're very pleased with him.' Dorcas looked at her enquiringly. 'That's good, isn't it?'

Philippa looked up, aware that a reply was required from her. 'Yes – yes, very.'

The other girl shook her head. 'You haven't a clue what I'm talking about, have you?' She leaned across the table. 'I was just saying how well Simon has been doing this term.' She looked at Philippa's plate. 'You've hardly touched your supper! What's the matter with you tonight, Pippa? You're miles away!'

When supper was over and the music started again John Dixon asked Philippa to dance. After that she danced with one or two other men, but at half past eleven she found herself suddenly yawning and thinking of Saturday morning's emergency surgery for which she would be on duty. She found Dorcas who was once again with John and made her excuses. John looked delighted.

'Don't worry, Philippa,' he said eagerly. 'I'll see that Dorcas gets home safe and sound.'

Dorcas said nothing, but glared at Philippa in a way that spoke volumes.

Collecting her coat, Philippa was making her way to the car park when she heard her name called and turned to see Brent hurrying towards her.

'You're not leaving, are you?' he asked. 'I've been working my way through my duty dances with all Aunt Angela's cronies. I'd thought you and I might have another before the evening was over.'

She smiled up at him. 'I thought it was time I called it a day. I'm on duty in the morning.'

He looked genuinely sorry. 'Oh – a pity.

Can I run you home?'

She shook her head. 'I have my car outside.'

He frowned. 'Of course. I should have realised.'

Philippa began to back away. 'Well, goodnight – and thanks.'

'Wait a minute!' He took a step towards her, closing the distance between them. 'Look, Philippa, if you're free tomorrow evening, I have two tickets for a concert over in Haythorpe.' He smiled. 'I know you like music. Would you like to go?'

She was taken aback. 'Well, I – yes, I think I can arrange that. May I let you know in the morning?'

He smiled. 'Of course. I'm not on duty, but I'll look in before surgery is over. See you then.'

Philippa turned up her coat collar against the chilly autumn air as she stepped out into the night. A date with Brent Charlesworth was the last thing she had expected to end this evening with, but the prospect lightened her heart and gave a spring to her step as she crossed the car park. What had happened to change his disapproval of her? she wondered.

CHAPTER FOUR

On Saturday mornings the surgery at the Health Centre was open for emergencies only. One of the partners was always available and there was always a nurse – now usually Philippa – on duty. On this particular morning they seemed to be more than usually busy and the small waiting room outside Philippa's room seemed full when she opened the door and asked for the first patient.

An elderly lady came into the room, accompanied by a younger one, who introduced herself immediately. 'Good morning, Nurse. I'm Mrs Carter and this is my mother, Mrs Haytor. Perhaps you know that she recently had an operation for the removal of a cataract to her right eye.'

Philippa looked at the elderly woman, who seemed rather ill at ease. 'Who is your doctor, Mrs Haytor?' she asked her.

'It's Doctor Frazer,' Mrs Carter broke in. She leaned forward. 'Mother's as deaf as a post, you won't make her hear you. She does have a deaf-aid, but will she wear it…?' She cast long-suffering eyes ceilingwards, leaving Philippa to draw her own conclusions. 'The thing is, you see,' she went on, 'I'm only here for the weekend, settling her in at home again, so to speak. She's been convalescing with me down in Worthing. And I thought it best to bring her along for advice while I'm here.'

'I see. So it isn't an emergency, then?' Philippa asked. 'Only, you see, strictly speaking Saturday mornings are reserved for emergency treatment.'

'I told her that, but she wouldn't listen!' It was the old lady who had spoken, and both looked at her in surprise.

Mrs Carter's smile vanished as she shot her mother a warning look, then, turning to Philippa, she mouthed the words: 'She lip-reads, you know – have to be careful.' Aloud, she said: 'It *is* an emergency in a way. You see, I'll be going home tomorrow and I did want to get things sorted out before I go.'

'Of course. I understand.' Philippa lifted the internal telephone and spoke to Jenny, asking for Mrs Haytor's notes to be brought in, then she looked at Mrs Carter again. 'Would you like to explain to me what the trouble is while we're waiting?' she asked.

Mrs Carter settled her large handbag more firmly on her lap and leaned forward, launching into her monologue in a sibilant stage whisper. 'Mother's operation wasn't very successful,' she began. 'It seems there's something wrong with the retina – that's at the back of the eye, you know – so taking the cataract off seems to have been rather a waste of time. Blind as a bat, she is.' She paused to glance round at her mother with a disapproving sniff. 'Well, *I* want her to come and live with us,' she went on. 'It's lovely down in Worthing. She'd be waited on hand and foot – have a room with a view of the sea – everything.' She gave a long-suffering sigh. 'But she just digs her heels in. All she wants is to come back here to that poky little bungalow in Heather Road.'

'Heather Road? That's just round the corner from where I live.' Philippa smiled at the old lady. 'I live quite near you, Mrs Haytor,' she said, trying to include the old lady in the conversation. As far as her daughter was concerned she might not have been there at all. Mrs Haytor responded to the smile readily and Philippa made a mental note that her sight wasn't all that bad.

Jenny came in with the notes and Philippa quickly scanned them, noting that what Mrs Carter said was, in fact, true. Her mother had no sight at all in her left eye, but she did have forty per cent in the right one. She looked up at the patient. 'How are you feeling after your operation, Mrs Haytor?' she asked. 'And how do you feel about coping on your own?'

The old lady smiled. 'I feel fine,' she said firmly, 'and it's wonderful to be home in my own place again.'

Her daughter looked scathing. 'Huh! That's all the thanks you get!' she said under her breath. Turning to her mother, she raised her voice. 'Don't be so independent, Mum. For a start off, you know you can't manage to put your eye-drops in, and anyway I'm afraid you might fall and hurt yourself. You could be lying there in a pool of blood for days before anyone found you – and me all those miles away!' She shook her head at Philippa. 'No consideration, old people, you know – none at all. All self!'

Appalled at the woman's insensitivity, Philippa addressed the old lady gently. 'Mrs Haytor, are you on the telephone?'

'Of course I am. And I'm not senile. I keep telling Maureen – I know my way round my own place, and I shall be all right.' She gave a short, derisive laugh. *'Lying-in-a-pool-of-blood* – rubbish!'

Mother and daughter exchanged hostile glances and Philippa smothered a smile. 'Well, I can easily arrange for the community nurse to visit you and help with your drops,' she said. 'And our social worker could look in and have a chat with you from time to time, just to make sure you're well and happy. Perhaps that would reassure you, Mrs Carter?'

The younger of the two women nodded grudgingly. Putting her hand up to shield her mouth, she hissed: *'What I really had in mind was a nice home.'*

'I've *got* a nice home,' Mrs Haytor put in. Her faded eyes twinkled at Philippa through her spectacles. 'You can come and have a cup of tea with me one day and see for yourself, dear, if you like.'

'Thank you. I might just do that, Mrs Haytor.' Philippa stood up. She knew there were other patients waiting and Mrs Carter seemed all set to sit there all morning. 'I wouldn't worry too much,' she advised, offering her hand to the woman. 'I'll see that someone keeps an eye on your mother. I don't think you have much to worry about.

Why not give her a month and see how she gets on?'

Mrs Carter wore an expression of extreme dissatisfaction as she reluctantly allowed herself to be ushered out, and Philippa drew a sigh of relief. She worked steadily through the rest of the patients, whose ailments consisted mainly of minor accidents, cuts and sprains. Only the last patient caused her any concern.

The man was about fifty and was accompanied by his wife. He looked pale and seemed short of breath. His wife spoke for him. 'He's had this pain all night, Nurse – right across his chest and down one arm. He didn't get any sleep.' She looked at her husband with concern and he tried to smile.

'I keep telling her, Nurse – I've had it before. No need to bother anyone about it. It's only a spot of indigestion.' But even as he spoke a spasm of pain crossed his face and he gasped for breath, clutching at his chest. Philippa picked up the telephone.

'Jenny, ask Doctor Frazer to come down here for a minute, will you, please – as quickly as he can?' She replaced the receiver and got up. 'Come and lie down on the couch for a moment, Mr...' She looked at the woman enquiringly.

'Simpson,' she supplied. 'Donald Simpson. We're patients of Doctor Frazer's, but we haven't seen him for ages. There's never been much wrong with Don – a really healthy man, he's always been.' She sat down, her hands twisting anxiously at the strap of her handbag.

Philippa worked quickly, raising the back rest of the examination couch and helping Mr Simpson on to it. She loosened his collar and the waistband of his trousers and picked up his wrist, feeling for the pulse. It was as she had expected, fast and erratic, and she noticed that there were beads of sweat breaking out on his forehead. She smiled at him reassuringly. 'Don't worry, Mr Simpson. Doctor Frazer will be here in a moment.'

The doctor arrived in seconds and made a brief examination of the man, then glancing at Philippa, he said: 'Get Jenny to telephone for an ambulance, will you? And I think we'll give him a spot of oxygen while we're waiting.'

Luckily Mr Simpson was the last patient of the morning, so when the ambulance arrived they were able to get him into it and off to hospital without any onlookers. As they watched it drive away Doctor Frazer turned to Philippa.

'A coronary. I dare say you've seen your share of those?'

She nodded. 'When I was working on Accident and Emergency we had quite a few. Poor man! He'd been kidding himself all last night that it was indigestion. If only he'd asked for help sooner!'

'That's a classic,' Doctor Frazer shook his head. 'But his chances are excellent. Castlebridge District has a very good heart unit. Ah, here's Doctor Charlesworth,' he remarked as Brent's dark blue Porsche drew up. 'What does he want, I wonder?' As Brent uncoiled his long length from the driving seat the older doctor called out jovially: 'What's the matter – can't you bear to be away from the place?'

Brent came up to them, smiling. 'I wanted a word with Nurse James.'

Doctor Frazer looked from one to the other, raising one eyebrow slightly as he noticed Philippa's heightened colour. 'Ah well, I'll leave you to it, then,' he said, walking back towards the building. 'See you later.'

Brent looked enquiringly at Philippa. 'What were you both doing out here?'

'We've just seen a patient off to hospital,'

she told him. 'A Mr Simpson – a coronary. Doctor Frazer seems to think he'll be all right, though.'

'Did he arrest?' asked Brent.

Philippa shook her head. 'No, thank goodness. Luckily there was a paramedic on the ambulance or I'd have gone with him just in case.'

She walked back inside the building, Brent following. In her room he closed the door and took a piece of paper out of his pocket. 'I thought you might like to see the programme for the concert tonight. They're playing Elgar's Second Symphony and the Brahms Violin Concerto.' He handed her the playbill and she studied it with interest.

'It sounds lovely.'

'So you'll come?'

Philippa hesitated. She had mentioned the invitation to Dorcas over breakfast and the other girl had said at once that she should go. She had no plans for this evening herself, so she would be there to be with Simon. It was just that she didn't understand the change of attitude on the part of Brent. Until last night he had been so distant and cool.

As though he read her thoughts he said: 'Please say yes. To be honest I feel that we rather got off on the wrong foot, and I'd like to put that right.'

'There's no need,' Philippa told him. 'Are you sure that the person you bought the ticket for doesn't want to go?' At the back of her mind she was thinking of the girl-friend Jenny had told her about – Emma something or other. Surely she must be back from her cruise by now.

'Sure,' Brent assured her. 'As a matter of fact I got the tickets as a surprise for Aunt Angela's birthday, but it seems she'd already arranged a dinner party.' He laughed. 'I suppose I should have known better than to try and surprise someone like her!'

'Well – if you're sure,' Philippa said slowly.

'Good. I'll pick you up around seven – maybe we could have a bite to eat afterwards too. See you later, then.'

When he had gone Philippa sat for a long time, trying to assess her feelings. It was so long since she had had a date – so long since she had felt this frisson of anticipation. Brent was undeniably attractive, and now that he had evidently overcome his initial resentment and disapproval he seemed to like her too. It would be all too easy to fall in love with a man like that, she told herself detachedly. But that was something she meant to guard against at all costs. She was as vulnerable as a schoolgirl after two years of being out of circulation. Peter's rejection had hurt her more deeply than she would ever admit, and she didn't intend to risk that again. Besides, there was Simon to consider now. A love affair could complicate her life in a way she wasn't yet ready to cope with. But as she tidied her room and prepared to go home she couldn't stop the flutter of excitement in the pit of her stomach at the thought of the evening ahead.

It was a really beautiful day, one of those warm golden autumn days that make winter seem a long way off. After lunch Dorcas suggested a picnic. Simon cheered up at the idea. Samantha had gone to visit her grandmother for the weekend and he was missing her.

'Can we go to the woods and look for blackberries?' he asked, jumping down from the table. 'Oh, please let's – *please!*'

Philippa laughed. 'All right, though I doubt if there'll be any left by now. You'd better put your wellies on – and an old sweater…' But he was already halfway up the stairs. Philippa looked at Dorcas. 'Well, it seems your suggestion has been adopted. Who's making the sandwiches – you or me?'

Dorcas grinned goodnaturedly. 'I'll do it,

you've been working all morning. You go and get some petrol while I see what we've got in the fridge.'

As it happened, Philippa was wrong about the blackberries; deep in the woods on the outskirts of Castlebridge, in a tangle of brambles where no one else had ventured, they found enough to fill their basket. Simon enjoyed himself, clambering to reach them, and by the time they got back to the car his mouth and fingers were stained a tell-tale purple.

'What shall we make with them?' he asked as he watched Dorcas stow the basket safely in the car boot.

'A pie, for tomorrow's lunch,' she replied. 'That's if they survive that long! Now, what about a game of football?' She produced a ball from the boot and threw it at him. He caught it and ran off, shouting with delight.

Philippa lay lazily on a rug on the grass and watched them, her eyes narrowed against the brilliance of the sunlight slanting through the branches above her. Dorcas had always been a tomboy at school and she hadn't changed at all. With her short hair, slim body and long legs encased in jeans, she might have been Simon's big brother as she raced across the grass and tackled him

84

for the ball. 'I'm so lucky to have found such a good friend,' Philippa told herself gratefully. Yet at the back of her mind she knew their situation was far from permanent. Dorcas was vital and attractive. Although she protested that another marriage was the last thing she wanted at the moment, Philippa felt that it was only a matter of time before another man entered her life; if not the faithful John Dixon, then someone equally adoring. Dorcas seemed to attract that kind of devotion in the opposite sex. She sighed and pushed the unwelcome notion of being alone again from her mind as she started to unpack the picnic basket.

By the time they got home Simon's eyes were heavy with tiredness and for once he didn't argue when Philippa said it was time for bed. Before he went to sleep he mentioned the pie Dorcas had said she'd make him, and Philippa promised to remind her. As she kissed him goodnight he said happily: 'Didn't we have a super time today? Pippa, are we always going to live with Dorcas?'

She considered for a moment. With Simon even more than most children the truth was essential. 'As far as I can see at the moment, darling,' she told him. 'But you can never really tell what might happen, can you?'

'No.' He looked at her for a long moment. 'A lot of things have happened to us, haven't they, Pippa?'

She nodded. 'Quite a lot – yes.'

Suddenly he threw his arms around her neck and hugged her hard. 'I love you, Pippa,' he whispered.

She settled him for sleep and switched out the light, pausing on the landing to think about what he had said. Simon badly needed to feel secure. Come to that, so did she. Being solely responsible for another person's happiness and security certainly made one mature faster than anything else she could think of. Sometimes she thought it was possibly one of the loneliest feelings in the world.

When she was ready Philippa announced her intention of going to the gate to wait for Brent. Dorcas looked at her critically.

'Why?' she asked. 'You're not ashamed of me, are you?'

Philippa laughed. 'Of course not! It's just that Simon's asleep and the doorbell might wake him.'

'Rubbish!' Dorcas said bluntly. 'You know damned well it's nothing of the kind. Have you told Brent about Simon, by the way?'

Philippa shook her head stubbornly. 'I told you before, Simon's my business. He's not something to be explained away to people.'

Dorcas sighed exasperatedly. 'Well, you know best. As you say, it's your business.'

It was a beautiful evening, still quite warm, with a thin mist rising from the fields after the day's heat. As Brent got out of the car and helped Philippa into the passenger seat he looked at his watch. 'Am I late?'

She shook her head. 'No. I was ready, so I thought I'd come out for a breath of air.'

He glanced at her as he fastened his seat-belt. 'You're looking very nice.'

She was wearing her grey suit again. Dorcas had remarked with characteristic candour that if she was going to start having a proper social life again it was time she bought herself some new clothes. She thanked Brent for the compliment, wondering yet again at his change of attitude towards her. The concert took place in Haythorpe's new riverside concert hall, and Philippa enjoyed it immensely. Music had always been evocative to her and as she listened to the nostalgic, heart-tugging strains of the Brahms Violin Concerto, her mind teemed with memories. How different her life was now! Over the last two years so much had happened. It seemed to her now that as a medical student she had been a totally different person – happy and carefree; not really knowing what life was all about. She had been deeply in love with Peter and when her brother had been killed, turning her life upside down, he had promised to stand by her: *'Somehow we'll weather the storm, Pippa. Don't worry, darling.'* She had believed him. It had never occurred to her not to. They had written every day and in those difficult, early days, his letters had been such a comfort. Then Peter had come to spend a weekend with them and been shocked at the extent of the responsibilities she had taken on. He had argued with her, begging her to make other arrangements and resume her own life again. By the time the weekend was over she had felt exhausted and torn in half. She had also known, deep inside, that there was no future in their relationship. She was right, his letters had gradually dwindled to one a week, then even less. There had been a subtle change in their tone too, until at last came the one she had been half expecting, yet dreading. It had been quite a kind letter, letting her down as lightly as possible. He had written of how much he admired her unselfish nature – her sacrifice; that he knew he would never have the strength of character to do the same – then he had broken the news of his engagement.

A storm of applause shattered Philippa's reverie and she joined in enthusiastically. Brent laid a hand on her arm.

'There's an interval of twenty minutes. Would you like a coffee or a drink?'

In the bar they found a corner table, and Philippa found him looking at her thoughtfully as she sipped her coffee.

'You *are* enjoying it, aren't you?' he asked.

She nodded. 'Oh yes. The orchestra's wonderful, and I've always wanted to see Andrew Medwin conduct.'

He raised an eyebrow at her. 'Then why did I catch you with tears in your eyes?'

She smiled selfconsciously. 'Music often affects me that way. It reminded me…'

'Of a lost love?' he asked perceptively.

Philippa shrugged. 'I was going to say – of happier days.' She took a deep drink of the hot coffee and looked at him. 'I think it's therapeutic to have a good wallow occasionally, don't you?'

For a long moment he looked into her eyes, until she blushed and looked away. 'Tell me about yourself, Philippa,' he said quietly. 'You know, you're rather an enigma.'

'I don't mean to be!' She looked up at

89

him. 'It's just that I can never see why my life should interest anyone else. Anyway, I told you all that you needed to know about me at the interview.'

'Point taken – if that was meant to put me in my place! I wasn't being nosey,' he explained. 'It's just that I like to know the people I work closely with, and I feel I know so little about you.'

She coloured. 'Of course, I'm afraid I must have sounded rude – I'm sorry.'

Brent smiled. 'Don't be. And don't feel you have to tell me anything unless you want to.'

'It was my sister-in-law I gave up my training to look after,' she said quickly. 'She and my brother were involved in a serious car accident two years ago. He was killed – she was paralysed, until she died of pneumonia six months ago.'

His hand reached impulsively for hers. 'Oh God! I'm sorry, Philippa.'

'I don't regret any of it, though at the time it meant giving up everything,' she went on without meeting his eyes. 'My career – my freedom...'

'And the man you loved?' he questioned.

She was acutely aware of the pressure of his fingers as she looked up and met his eyes. 'I – suppose you could say that.' She shrugged, laughing lightly. 'I'm a fatalist, though. I can see now that it would have been a serious mistake. Sometimes these things work out for the best.'

'But now that you're alone again...' Brent went on, 'surely you could pick up where you left off – with your career, I mean?'

Philippa hesitated. Should she tell him about Simon? She decided against it. On top of the other things she had told him it sounded too much like a hard luck story, and she was sick and tired of people feeling sorry for her. Simon needed her so much, and in a different way she needed him too. She was damned if she'd have people thinking he was some kind of burden to her. 'I'm different now,' she told him truthfully. 'An experience like that changes you. I'm not sure that I want the same things any more. I don't have the same values. I feel I need time to readjust.'

He nodded understandingly. 'I can imagine...' The bell signalling the start of the second half of the concert rang and he got to his feet, holding out his hand to her with a smile. 'Come on – the Elgar will put you in a happier mood, then we'll go somewhere and eat our heads off.'

He was right about the Elgar symphony. Its sweeping harmonies seemed to lift her on to a higher plane. As they came out into the cool night air Brent took her arm. 'We can leave the car here and walk to the restaurant. It's just a little further down the river.'

The riverbank was fringed with willows, a few dry leaves still clinging to the branches that swept low over the water. Silver in the moonlight, they rustled softly, brushing the surface of the water with a quiet lapping sound. Brent's arm fell across her shoulders, his hand cupping her shoulder, drawing her closer to his side.

'I was wrong about you, Philippa,' he said quietly.

She looked up at him. 'How – wrong?'

'I thought you were arrogant – cagey and defensive because you'd given up medicine. I thought you considered yourself a cut above an everyday nurse.' He looked down at her. 'I'm afraid I must have been unbearable to work with.'

She laughed. 'Only *slightly* unbearable!'

Brent winced. 'I'm sorry. I admit that I was against your appointment at first.' He stopped and turned her towards him, his hands on her shoulders. 'You're an excellent nurse, though; calm – perceptive, efficient. We couldn't have chosen better.' He looked into her eyes. 'So do you forgive me?'

'Of course.' She smiled up into the blue eyes.

'Your period of readjustment is definitely our gain.' He returned her gaze. 'I expect I'm selfish to hope it will last for a while yet,' he told her. 'And if you need any help or advice...'

'Thanks – it's very good of you.' For a moment they stood looking at each other, then, feeling slightly embarrassed, Philippa searched her mind for a casual remark that would break the silence. 'Brent – I...' Her words were cut off as his mouth closed over hers. It was a gentle kiss, but it seemed to stop the world from turning just for a split second. As their lips parted she looked up at him. 'Please, I...' But when his arms tightened round her, drawing her closer, she gave up her struggle to fight against what she was feeling. This time his lips were firmer, demanding the response she was trying so hard to hold back. With a small shock she realised that she had wanted him to kiss her like this for some time. At last he released her. Cupping her chin, he tilted her face upwards, his candid blue eyes searching hers questioningly.

At last she pushed him gently away, shivering slightly.

'You're cold,' he said, clasping her cool fingers in his warm, firm hand. 'Let's go and eat. That's the restaurant over there.'

Over the meal they talked about the counselling clinic, and Philippa found herself becoming more and more interested in the idea. Brent told her some of the amusing things that had happened to him during his training and they exchanged anecdotes. Gradually she relaxed, enjoying his company and losing some of her inhibitions. She found herself laughing, seeing a lighter side of him, a sense of humour that matched her own. As they tried to attract the attention of the waiter to ask for more coffee, she studied his face; the firm chin and high cheekbones, the deep-set eyes and thick fair hair. He turned back, caught her looking at him and covered her hand with his.

'I've enjoyed this evening very much, Philippa,' he said softly.

She was about to reply when an excited female voice cut in: 'Brent! So this is where you are. I've been ringing your flat all evening!'

Philippa turned to see an extremely pretty

blonde girl standing by their table. She was elegantly dressed in a black dress, an expensive-looking fox jacket draped carelessly over her shoulders. Her blue eyes gazed adoringly at Brent. 'I got back last night,' she told him. 'Auntie and I got off the boat at Las Palmas and spent a few days there – flew home yesterday. How are you, sweetie? I've been longing to see you and tell you all about the trip.' She pouted. 'I did think you might have rung…'

'I'm fine.' Brent stood up and pulled out a chair. 'Do sit down, Emma. Perhaps you'd like some coffee. I'd like you to meet Philippa James. She's our new nurse/receptionist at the Health Centre.' He turned to Philippa. 'Philippa, this is Emma Francis. Her father is a friend of Greg Frazer's.'

Emma looked rather surprised at Brent's way of introducing her, but she smiled at Philippa and offered her hand. 'Hello, nice to meet you. Are you enjoying working for old sobersides here?'

Philippa smiled. 'I like working at the Health Centre very much, thanks.'

The other girl laughed, dimpling with delight. 'How diplomatic!' She looked at Brent. 'I can tell you've got a real gem here.' Something in Brent's expression wiped the smile from her face, replacing it with a look of anxious hurt. 'Oh, I didn't think – I'm not butting in, am I?' She looked at Philippa. 'You must forgive me. Brent and I have known each other since ever and when I saw him I was so pleased I just had to come across and say hello.' She glanced at Brent through lowered lashes, then, sensing his annoyance, rose awkwardly to her feet. 'Oh well, this won't do, will it?' she said with a little laugh. 'I'd better get back to my own table. My friends will be wondering where I've got to.'

When she had gone Philippa glanced at Brent. His mouth had taken on a hard, closed look. He stared back unsmilingly at her, beckoning the waiter. 'Perhaps we'd better go. It's getting late.'

Gathering her bag and gloves, she nodded. Somehow the relaxed feeling had gone and it was as though the barrier was up between them again. Her heart sank. Surely there was no need for Brent to be quite so unkind to the girl – unless... She pushed the suspicion from her mind as she allowed herself to be ushered out of the restaurant. Nevertheless, the evening was quite spoilt.

CHAPTER FIVE

In the car on the way home Brent made only the briefest reference to Emma's appearance at the restaurant. 'Emma is a very old friend, as she told you,' he said, his eyes on the road as he edged the car out of the crowded car park. 'She's just come back from a world cruise with an aunt who happens to be one of Aunt Angela's oldest friends.'

Philippa made a polite remark and the subject was closed, but the tense atmosphere in the car told her that the episode had caused him some discomfort. He was silent, and stealing a look at his profile etched against the car window, Philippa saw that his mouth was still set in that hard line and there was a closed, withdrawn look about his eyes. When they drew up outside the house he switched off the engine and turned to her.

'Thank you for coming out with me this evening, Philippa. I hope you enjoyed it as much as I did.'

'I did – very much,' she said. Suddenly it seemed they were back where they started. The warmth and closeness they had shared earlier might have all been in her imagination. Brent smiled at her, but his eyes were still far away – with Emma perhaps?

'Good.' He got out of the car and came round to her side, opening the door for her and helping her out. As they stood on the pavement together, his hand still holding her arm, he said: 'We must do this again some time. Goodnight, Philippa.'

She felt her cheeks burning. The remark sounded as though he thought it was expected of him. Did he think she was waiting for him to ask her for another date – to kiss her again? She turned abruptly. 'Goodnight, Brent – and thank you.' She opened the gate and slipped inside, running up the path to the front door without a backward glance – fumbling in her bag for her door key.

At the gate he watched, an enigmatic expression on his face, then he too turned, got into the car and drove off into the night.

'Well, how did it go?' Dorcas looked up from the settee where she was sitting with her feet up, watching the TV. As she saw the expression on Philippa's face her jaw dropped. 'Ah! I see I shouldn't have asked. Sparks still flying, are they?'

Philippa sighed and lifted her shoulders. 'We had a lovely evening. The concert was sheer magic, the meal great. Everything was wonderful until...'

'Don't tell me – one of your false eyelashes fell in the soup!'

Philippa dropped into a chair, impervious to Dorcas's attempt to lighten her depression. 'Nothing so trivial.' She looked at her friend. 'Emma Francis suddenly turned up. She's been away on a three-month world cruise. Jenny Wishart told me about her. Apparently she's Brent's girl-friend.'

Dorcas snorted. 'Huh! Going on three-month cruises hardly seems the ideal way to keep your man!' she shrugged. 'Maybe their affair was falling apart anyway. But whichever way you look at it she could hardly expect him to sit twiddling his thumbs, waiting for her to come home, could she?'

'I think she probably did,' Philippa said glumly. 'And what's more, I wouldn't mind betting that Brent led her to believe he would. It was quite clear that he was taken aback by meeting her unexpectedly like that. She obviously adores him, too.'

'Spoilt kids always expect to get their own

way,' Dorcas remarked.

Philippa looked up. 'You know her?'

'Only vaguely. Her father's a solicitor –
and on the board of governors at school.
Emma's mother died when she was quite
small and Daddy's never stopped trying to
make up to her for it.' She looked thoughtful
for a moment. 'Maybe the cruise was an
attempt to smarten Brent's ideas up; bring
him up to scratch. Absence makes the heart
grow fonder – all that stuff.'

Philippa shrugged. 'And maybe it worked!
Seeing her obviously gave him something to
think about, not to mention putting the
damper on our evening. He hardly spoke a
word afterwards.'

Dorcas looked closely at her. 'Does it
matter a lot to you? I mean, you're not
falling for him, are you?'

Philippa forced a laugh. 'Good heavens,
no! I'm like you; I can do without that kind
of complication in my life at the moment.
It's just that...' She trailed off lamely,
unable to find the words to describe what
she felt – not even sure herself.

Dorcas rose to her feet, stretching her arms
above her head and yawning. 'Aah – thank
goodness it's Sunday tomorrow!' She smiled
sympathetically at Philippa. 'Nothing we can

do about it, love. Tell you what – I'll make you a nice cup of cocoa.'

Monday brought a change in the weather. Philippa woke to the sound of rain drumming against her windowpane. Simon opened her bedroom door and peered round it.

'What's the time?'

Philippa looked at her bedside clock. 'It's only seven. Needn't get up just yet.'

'Can I get in with you? I'm cold.' He crept in beside her and snuggled close. 'We're having pairing day at school this week,' he informed her. 'Will you come?'

She looked at him. 'Pairing day? Oh, you mean *parents*' day. Yes, of course I'm coming. I hope you've got lots of nice work to show me.'

He nodded eagerly. 'Yes. We all had to draw a picture of our family. I drew you and Dorcas.'

Philippa held her breath, waiting for him to ask the inevitable question, but he hurried on: 'We've got rabbits and a hamster at school too. You'll like them, Pippa– Pippa...'

'Yes?'

'If I ask you something, you won't say no, will you?'

'It depends,' she said cautiously. 'What is it?'

'Can I have a dog?' He sat up and looked intently into her face, his expression heart-rendingly pleading. 'Please let me, Pippa – *please!*'

She sighed. 'Darling, it wouldn't be fair. We're out all day and a dog would get lonely. Besides, this isn't our house. Dorcas might not like it.'

His face crumpled with disappointment. 'Maybe I could take it to school. It could play with the other animals.'

'It wouldn't be allowed, I'm afraid,' she told him.

'If I asked – and if Dorcas said we could...' His bright eyes searched hers hopefully.

Sadly, Philippa shook her head. 'We could have a hamster,' she suggested.

'I don't want a hamster. You can't take them for walks and play ball with them. Samantha's got a dog. He's called Bob and he's big, but we could have just a little one if you like. Can we, Pippa? *Can* we?'

She pulled him close. 'We'll have to see,' she told him. 'We'll talk to Dorcas about it, but I told you – leaving a dog shut up by itself all day would be cruel, and you wouldn't want that, now would you?'

It was a bad start, and right from that moment it promised to be 'one of those days'. To begin with she had trouble starting the Mini and arrived at the Health Centre ten minutes later than usual. As she hurriedly changed into her uniform, she noticed the notes she had left on her desk on Saturday, reminding her to notify Nick Cornish and Daphne Walsh, the community nurse, about Mrs Haytor. Hurriedly she fastened her belt and went out to Reception.

'Jenny, have the nurses been in?' she asked. But at that moment the door opened and Daphne Walsh came bustling in, her navy mac dripping with rain and her round face whipped pink by the cold air. She grinned cheerfully at Philippa.

'Morning. Looks as though the weather's had its fling, doesn't it?'

Philippa gave a sigh of relief. 'I'm glad I've caught you. I don't know whether you've been notified, but Mrs Haytor is home.' She fumbled in her pocket. 'I've got her address here somewhere.'

'Don't worry, I've got it,' Daphne told her. 'I thought she was with her daughter, though.'

'She was. I don't think they were getting on too well,' Philippa explained. 'They came to see me on Saturday morning. Mrs Haytor wants to stay in her own house, but her daughter was talking about finding a place for her in a home.'

Daphne sighed. 'Oh dear, the old story. Don't worry, I'll look in on her this morning. I expect she'll be needing someone to help with her eye-drops if she's on her own.' She turned to Jenny. 'Now, are there any more messages for me?'

Philippa went along the corridor and tapped on the door of the social worker's office. Nick Cornish called out a cheery 'Come in' and she opened it to find him sitting at his desk working on a brightly coloured poster.

'I'm glad I've caught you,' she said. 'There's someone I'd like you to keep an eye on...'

Nick looked up with his boyish grin. 'What do you think of this?' He held up the poster. It announced the meeting to discuss the counselling clinic, the date for which she saw had been fixed for Thursday of that week. She smiled. 'You've made a good job of it. It should certainly catch the eye with all those bright colours.'

'That's what I thought.' He stood up, picking up a box of drawing pins and slipping them into the pocket of his jeans. 'I'll just put it up on the waiting room notice board before the rush starts.' He looked at her. 'Oh, sorry – what was it you wanted?'

She told him briefly about Mrs Haytor, gave him the address and went back to her own room.

The morning was fairly routine until, just as Philippa was seeing her last patient out, she heard a child crying in Reception. A moment later Jenny came in.

'There's a woman out there with a little boy,' she said. 'He's screaming his head off and it looks as though he's injured his leg quite badly. Both doctors are busy with patients at the moment. Could you have a look?'

'Of course, bring her in.'

Jenny ushered in a young woman carrying a little boy of about four. He was very distressed and Philippa saw immediately that he was in shock. 'Lay him on the couch,' she told his mother. She saw that the child's right thigh was badly swollen and discoloured and that the leg rolled ominously outwards. 'Fractured femur', her mind registered. She looked at the woman. 'What's his name?'

The young woman moistened her lips

nervously. 'Wayne – will he be all right? Can't you give him something to help the pain?'

Philippa stroked the little boy's cheek. 'Try to keep still, Wayne. We'll make the pain go away soon.' She looked at the mother. 'How did it happen?'

'He was playing on the stairs and he slipped. He landed awkwardly.' The girl was obviously upset and desperately worried. Her face was deathly pale and her hands trembled as she fumbled in her bag for a handkerchief. Philippa smiled reassuringly at her and pulled up a chair. 'Sit down a moment. Stay with him. I'll be right back,' she told her. Slipping into Reception again, she said to Jenny: 'The minute one of the doctors is free, ask him to come to my room. I think we've got a fractured femur. You'd better ring for an ambulance too while you're about it.'

She was gently examining the small boy when the door opened and Brent came in. 'Good morning, Nurse. I hear we have an emergency.' Philippa moved aside for him, briefly telling him all she knew of the patient's history. After a brief examination he turned to her.

'I think we'll give him a whiff of gas for the pain while I immobilise the leg. Have you sent for an ambulance?' She nodded, turning away to get the emergency Entonox equipment. Brent looked at the mother. 'I'm afraid your little boy has fractured his femur – that's the thigh-bone. He'll have to go to hospital, but don't worry, you can go with him and stay there too if you can arrange things at home.'

'But won't he be able to come home with me once they've put it in plaster?' she asked.

Brent shook his head. 'I'm afraid a fracture of the femur means he'll have to be in traction for several weeks,' he told her gently. He patted her shoulder. 'Don't worry. He's a strong little fellow. You'll be surprised at how quickly he gets used to being in hospital.' He deftly splinted and bandaged the injured leg while Philippa administered the mixture of oxygen and nitrous oxide, encouraging the little boy to breathe with her. The ambulance arrived and they saw the child and his mother into it. As it drove away Brent turned to her. 'Poor little chap. He's in for a long spell in hospital, I'm afraid.' He sighed. 'I'm afraid she'll be in for some close questioning when they get there too. It's hard, I know, but we can't be too careful where child injuries are concerned nowadays. It's one of the darker facts of life.'

Philippa was silent, her sympathy with the child's mother – thinking of Simon and how she would be feeling in similar circumstances. Brent looked closely at her.

'Are you all right?'

She forced a smile. 'Yes – of course.'

He looked thoughtful for a moment. 'Injured children always affect one more,' he said. 'They seem so defenceless. They're a lot tougher than they look, though. Take my word for it.' He looked at his watch. 'Good heavens! Look at the time. I'm going to be behind all day if I don't get a move on. See you later.'

In the office there was a welcome cup of coffee ready and Philippa sat down to enjoy it.

'Are you all right?' asked Jenny. 'You're looking a bit pale this morning.'

'I'm fine,' Philippa told her.

Jenny gave her a speculative, sideways glance and asked mischievously: 'Have a nice evening out on Saturday?'

Philippa looked up in surprise. 'Yes, thank you. But how did you…?'

'Ah, a little bird told me that a certain good-looking young doctor took you out!' Jenny giggled. 'Not much I don't hear about.

Anyway, I'd guessed he might be about to ask you.'

'Oh, really? And what made you think that?'

Jenny fed a piece of paper into her typewriter and began tapping away. 'Oh, just that I heard Doctor Frazer talking to him on Friday afternoon,' she said. 'He was telling him he ought to be nicer to you – oh, not that I was listening, of course. I just sort of overheard them when I was getting the room ready for the meeting.' She peered at the handwritten letter she was typing. 'Really! Doctor Copeland's writing gets worse! Is that an M or a W, I wonder?'

Philippa's mind was spinning. 'Doctor Frazer…'

'No, Doctor *Copeland.*' Jenny pushed the letter across the desk towards her. 'Can *you* read it?'

'I was talking about what you just said – about Doctor Frazer telling Brent – Doctor Charlesworth to be nicer to me. I'd like to know what he said, if you don't mind.'

Jenny stopped peering at the letter and looked up, her jaw dropping in dismay. 'Oh hell! I've put my foot in it, haven't I?'

Philippa's heart was thudding uncomfortably. 'Well, come on. You've said so much, you might as well tell me all of it now.' She wasn't at all sure that she wanted to hear what was coming. She only knew she had to know the truth.

Jenny hedged. 'It was nothing really – just that Doctor Frazer seemed to think he was being a bit hard on you.' She peered anxiously at Philippa. 'Well, he *was*, wasn't he? Doctor Frazer said that good nurses were hard to find and it would be a pity if you were to leave because you weren't happy.'

Philippa was silent. So *that* was why he'd been so charming to her on Friday evening at the school dance – and why he'd invited her to the concert and dinner – as a kind of *duty!* She'd wondered at his change of attitude. Well, now she knew the answer. Surely he hadn't needed to go to the lengths he had though? Suddenly she remembered their encounter with Emma Francis at the restaurant. No wonder he had been so silent on the way home. Obviously he would find it particularly galling, having to offer Emma the unlikely explanation that he was merely doing his public relations bit!

Jenny looked at her with an agonised expression. 'Philippa, you're not upset, are you? Oh, *why* can't I learn to keep my big mouth shut?'

Philippa shook her head. 'Don't worry. It's not important. Anyway, Doctor Charlesworth should be in a better mood now. I hear his girl-friend is back from her jet-setting holiday.'

'Emma? You don't say!' Jenny's eyes brightened. 'How did you hear…?'

Philippa stood up. She had to escape before Jenny wheedled any more information out of her. She looked at her watch. 'Just look at the time! I'd better go and tidy my room. See you later, Jenny.'

The receptionist part of Philippa's duties consisted of standing in for Jenny during the afternoons. It was the quietest part of the day and there was little to do except man the telephone and deal with patients who came in for repeat prescriptions and to make appointments. It was almost four o'clock and she was just looking out patients' cards for evening surgery when someone walked into the office. She turned from the filing cabinet, and was startled to find herself face to face with Brent.

'Oh!' The tray containing the cards slipped from her hands to the floor with a clatter and she sank to her knees, scooping them up, dismayed that they were now in a

111

complete muddle.

'Here, let me help you.'

She looked up to find Brent's face close to hers as he crouched beside her, helping to gather up the scattered cards. 'It's quite all right,' she told him stiffly. 'I can manage.'

'I'm sorry if I startled you?'

She stood up and put the cards on the desk, starting to sort them out, appalled at the quickened beating of her heart.

He handed her the cards. 'Are you free next Friday?' he asked. 'I thought…'

'It's all right. You don't have to!' She turned to face him, her eyes bright and her cheeks flushed. 'You apologised very nicely for being offhand with me and it's forgotten. There's no need to make yourself a permanent martyr!'

His brows came together in a frown. 'What are you talking about?'

Philippa turned away with a shrug, her fingers trembling as she fumbled with the cards. 'Doctor Frazer asked you to make an effort, didn't he? Well, you made it. Thanks!'

There was a pause, then she found her shoulders grasped in a iron grip as Brent turned her roughly to face him. 'Now just you listen to me a minute. What do you think I am, the office boy or something?' His eyes blazed into hers and she noticed in an oddly detached way that there were tiny green flecks in them that seemed to intensify when he was angry. 'All right, so I wasn't particularly friendly when you first came here, but I'd already decided I was wrong about you. Maybe Greg did mention it, but that wasn't why I asked you out.'

Philippa was riveted by the intensity of his eyes as they blazed into hers. She was aware of his fingers bruising her shoulders too, but somehow she couldn't find the strength to pull away.

Suddenly he gave a shout of exasperated laughter. 'Good God, Philippa! Surely you didn't imagine I'd go to those lengths for the good of the practice, did you?'

'W-what lengths?' she asked weakly.

For a moment he searched her eyes, then he pulled her to him and kissed her hard. '*Those* lengths, idiot,' he said as their lips parted. 'I asked you out because I *wanted* to. I kissed you because I wanted to, and I'd very much like to go on doing it, if you've no objection.' He drew her closer, but she held herself rigid within the circle of his arms as she asked:

'What about your friend – Emma? I thought – I thought I might have spoiled

113

things for you.'

He held her away from him for a moment. 'Someone been filling you in on that too? It so happens that that particular episode in my life was over a long time ago, but that's another story. Look, come out with me on Friday and we'll talk.'

She was about to give in and agree when she remembered that Friday was parents' day at the school. 'Not Friday,' she told him, shaking her head. 'I...' Suddenly someone tapped sharply on the glass window that separated the office from the reception area and a voice called out: '*Shop!*'

Philippa sprang back guiltily and spun round to see Nick Cornish's freckled face grinning at her. 'Oh! It's you, Nick,' she said shakily.

'Good job it *is* only me,' he remarked under his breath as Brent walked swiftly out of the office and brushed past him without a glance. 'Naughty goings on at the Health Centre! What *would* the patients say?'

Philippa cleared her throat, blushing with embarrassment. 'It – wasn't anything of the kind,' she told him defensively. 'Doctor Charlesworth was telling me – about...' But Nick's laugh silenced her.

'I *bet* he was! No need to explain. I can be

quite bright sometimes.' He grinned at her. 'And don't worry, I won't breathe a word. Now, I really wanted to speak to you about this old dear – Mrs Haytor. I'm going out that way now and I thought I'd pop in.'

The rest of the week lived up to Monday's promise and Philippa hardly had a moment to herself. She saw little of Brent until the meeting on Thursday evening. All the staff of the Health Centre turned out, even Gladys, who served coffee and biscuits during the break halfway through, when everyone gathered in groups to discuss the idea that had been put to them. By the end of the meeting it had been agreed that one clinic a month should be held until they saw how great the demand was. But there was little doubt that the patients thought it a good idea. Of course there was the odd exception, one of whom was Gladys, who made her views abundantly clear over the washing up. Jenny and Philippa had stayed behind to help her with this as they were all giving up an evening on a voluntary basis.

She sniffed disapprovingly as she swished her washing-up mop vigorously round the bowl. 'Never did hold with washing dirty linen in public!' she announced suddenly.

Philippa and Jenny exchanged glances. 'I hadn't visualised it quite like that,' said Philippa. 'After all, it isn't exactly "in public", as you say. The idea is for people to use their personal experience to help each other, but anything really personal could be discussed privately. We thrashed all that out at the meeting.'

'I know all that,' Gladys said stubbornly. 'And I *still* don't hold with it. I've always believed in independence meself. You makes your own trouble and you gets yourself out of it the best you can.'

'But what if you can't?' asked Jenny. 'What if you've no one to turn to? There are an awful lot of lonely, worried people around who must ache for someone to tell their troubles to. I read where nine-tenths of today's illnesses are psychosomatic.'

Gladys gave a derisive grunt. 'Trendy claptrap, if you ask me!' she announced. 'What *I* says is that you makes your bed and you lies on it – come what may!' And by the look on her face both girls knew there was little point in arguing with her on the subject.

When she had gone Jenny pulled on her coat and glanced at Philippa. 'Are you coming my way? I'll make you a coffee if you like. I'm thinking of decorating my bedsit and I'd like your opinion on some wallpaper books I've got.'

Philippa looked at her watch and shook her head. 'I won't tonight, Jenny, if you don't mind. I've got some supplies in my room to unpack. They came this morning and I haven't had a minute to put them away.'

She heard the others leaving as she unpacked the box of sterile dressings and disposable syringes, putting them away in the cupboard. She was just folding the cardboard box flat when the door opened and Brent looked round it.

'Still here?'

'Yes.' She indicated the box. 'Some stuff that arrived this morning. This is the first chance I've had to put it away.'

He smiled. 'Come and have a drink.'

Philippa looked doubtfully at her watch. Every night this week Simon had been in bed by the time she got home. Tonight would be no exception. But it was too late to worry about it now, it was already well past his bedtime. 'All right,' she agreed.

As Brent set the burglar alarm and locked the door securely he glanced at her. 'Is that friend of yours nervous of being alone?' he asked.

117

'No – why?'

He took her arm as they headed for the car park. 'Just that you always seem in such a hurry to get home.' He slipped an arm casually round her shoulders and looked down at her. 'I shall soon begin to suspect you of having a husband tucked away,' he joked.

They went to the Boar's Head, a little pub on the outskirts of Castlebridge. It was crowded with the usual rather noisy Friday evening clientele, but they found a table close to the inglenook fireplace. Brent looked at Philippa.

'I think the meeting went well.'

'Yes. I'm sure the idea will take off.' She sipped her sherry and found herself beginning to relax – until she realised he was looking at her, a speculative expression in his eyes.

'Tell me about yourself, Philippa,' he invited.

She stiffened. 'I already did – the other evening.'

He shook his head. 'You told me about your circumstances. This time I want to hear about *you*. What do you intend to do with your life, for instance? Where do you go from here? I mean, nurse/receptionist at the

Centre is hardly a career, is it? And now that you're free again…'

Philippa looked into her glass. 'I told you, I want to think things out – readjust my life. At the moment I'm taking life one day at a time.'

'Nevertheless, you must have *some* idea of what you want.'

'Not particularly.' She shrugged, beginning to feel uncomfortable. What right had he to push her into a corner like this? She looked up, meeting his eyes in an unspoken challenge. 'What about you? What do *you* plan to do with your life?'

His eyes registered surprise and he looked thoughtful as he said: 'There was a time when I'd have liked to specialise in obstetrics, but I feel I've left it a bit late.' He took a long pull of his beer. 'Anyway, I like Castlebridge,' he told her. 'All my friends and what family I have are here; general practice suits me. I get along well with my partners…'

'In other words, you're in a comfortable rut!'

He met her eyes, his eyebrows rising. 'And *that* makes two of us, wouldn't you say?'

They laughed together and the tension between them relaxed a little as he said:

119

'That's better. It's nice to see you laugh. You're rather a tense little person, aren't you? And that reminds me – you were about to tell me about your plans.'

Philippa bit her lip. Her neat little diversion had failed. The ball was back in her court again. She was just about to try another tack when a tall young man guffawed loudly and stepped backwards, knocking clumsily into their table. Brent gave her a wry smile.

'I think it's time to go.'

Outside in the car park he took her arm and turned her towards him. 'It's still quite early. Come back to the flat, and I'll make you a sandwich – I'm famous for them.'

She shook her head, feeling a sudden stab of panic. 'I can't.'

'Why not? Just give me one good reason!' he demanded.

She shrugged, at a loss.

He took her arm decisively. 'We'll go in my car. I'll drive you back here to get yours later.'

Philippa was silent as they drove. He seemed determined to find out all about her, and suddenly she was afraid. It was so long since she had confided in a man. Peter had thought her mad to take on what he considered an 'unnecessary responsibility'. He had clearly despised her for giving up her future career to look after someone else's child. Perhaps Brent would see it in the same light. In any event, he would wonder why she had never mentioned Simon before. She slumped wearily in her seat, and when Brent drew the car to a halt outside an elegant Regency house on the riverside it was an effort for her to get out and walk with him to the front entrance. She wished with all her heart that she'd had the will to say 'no'.

CHAPTER SIX

Brent's flat occupied the first floor of the eighteenth-century terraced house. In the lounge, two floor-length windows looked out on to the river. An elegant marble fireplace was flanked by arched recesses, lined with bookshelves. A velvety green carpet covered the floor and the twin settees flanking the fireplace were of soft buttoned hide in a pale beige colour.

Brent switched on a large cream-shaded table lamp and crossed the room to draw the curtains. He turned to Philippa with a smile. 'Welcome to my retreat.'

She looked around her admiringly. 'It's charming.'

He smiled. 'Thanks. I like it too. I only wish I got to see more of it.' He held out his hand for her coat. 'Now, what will you have? I can do ham, cold beef, tomato…'

'Nothing, thanks. I'm not hungry.'

'Coffee, then?'

Philippa didn't really want a coffee either, but she smiled and nodded politely.

'Thank you.'

While Brent was away she wandered round the room, looking at its contents, noting the small things that gave her clues about Brent's lifestyle and his personality. On a small glass-topped table was a photograph of him as a schoolboy with a woman Philippa recognised as a younger Angela Stone. Facing it was another photograph, this time of an attractive, smartly dressed blonde woman with sharp, intelligent features. She picked it up to look more closely. There was a strong resemblance between her and the young boy in the other photograph.

'My mother,' Brent confirmed for her as he came in carrying a tray. He elbowed the door shut. 'That was taken soon after she took over the family business. She was – and *is* – quite the lady tycoon.'

Philippa put the photograph down and crossed the room to sit down. Brent had put the tray down on the coffee table between the settees and was pouring. 'What sort of business is it?' she asked as she took a seat opposite him.

He handed her a cup. 'Haulage. Maybe you've heard of Charlesworth Expressline.'

She had. Their distinctive brown and cream vehicles were to be seen on every road in the country. She stared at him. 'You mean your mother runs that?'

He laughed dryly. 'She does. Quite an achievement for a woman, so I'm told.'

Philippa was impressed. 'I should say so! You must be very proud of her.'

He hesitated just a fraction too long before saying: 'Yes – yes, of course I am.' He took a sip of his coffee and looked at her. 'Now, about this notion you seem to have picked up that I was told to "make an effort to be nice to you"...'

Philippa blushed with embarrassment. 'Oh, please forget I said that.'

'I'm afraid I can't.' He put his cup down and looked at her gravely. 'It came from Jenny, of course. I remember her hovering at the time Greg and I were having that particular conversation.' He smiled disarmingly. 'Tell me the truth – did you really think I was merely doing as I was told?'

Philippa squirmed. 'Please – can't we talk about something else?'

'I'm afraid we can't.' He got up and came round the table to join her on the facing settee. 'If Jenny had hung around for a few minutes longer she would have heard the rest of the conversation,' he told her. 'She would, for instance, have heard me telling

Greg that I was delighted with the way you fitted in at Castlebridge Health Centre, also how wrong I'd been in my initial judgement.' She opened her mouth to protest, but he held up his hand. 'Wait – hear me out, Philippa. I realise that all that sounds pompous and patronising. It's just that I want you to know that I don't mind admitting that I can make mistakes, like anyone else. But none of that had any bearing on my decision to ask you out. That was done for very different reasons.'

'Oh?' She lifted her coffee cup and hid her face in it, trying not to let him see the colour that flooded her cheeks.

Brent smiled. 'Don't you want to hear what they were?' He put out a hand to take the cup from her and put it on the table. As he did so his fingers brushed her arm and she felt her skin tingle under his touch. 'I'm sorry, I'm only teasing you really,' he told her gently. He moved closer to her, taking her hand. 'I'll put my cards on the table. I've never cared much for ambitious women. However, having said that I also despise people who give up too easily. For that reason I jumped to the mistaken conclusion that you were a bit of a phoney; that, having opted out of medicine – apparently because you couldn't cope – you were likely to be on the defensive about it.' He smiled wryly at her. 'And I think you must admit that at first that's the impression you gave.'

Philippa turned to him indignantly. 'If I did, it was because you were always trying to make me look small. I had to defend myself. Surely you realised that? I do have my pride.'

'I know that, and I admire you for it.' He squeezed her hand gently. 'Just as I know and admire a lot of other things about you now that we've worked together. I also know that I behaved like a boor. I wanted to show you that I could be different.'

'I see. There was really no need, though – I mean – it doesn't matter...' Philippa broke off, confused and suddenly tongue-tied.

'Oh, but it does. It matters rather a lot to me, Philippa,' he insisted. 'I've found myself wondering about you – wanting to get to know you better.' He cupped her chin, turning her face towards him. 'Surely you don't object to that?'

Of course she didn't. Hadn't she felt exactly the same herself? But she couldn't find the words to tell him, instead she nodded, her mouth dry and her throat constricting as his eyes searched hers.

Suddenly his mouth curved into a smile.

'Don't look at me like that! I'm not going to eat you!' He shook his head. 'That's one of the things that puzzles me about you, Philippa. You seem so cool and in command in some ways, yet I can feel you withdraw when I try to get close to you. I know there was once a man in your life – someone important. Did he hurt you badly – do you want to talk about it?'

Philippa moved away slightly, her heart thudding uneasily. 'No. It was over long ago and we parted quite amicably. I think I told you – it would never have worked out.'

Brent reached out to take her hand again, preventing her from moving further away. 'Tell me the truth, Philippa – are you still in love with him?' His face was very close to hers and she looked into the blue-green eyes and found herself drowning in their depths.

'No,' she whispered.

'I see – so it can't be that.' His lips found hers, very gently at first, experimentally – sensuously brushing as though to test her receptiveness. The breath caught in her throat and his arms encircled her, drawing her close as his mouth grew harder, more searching. Her arms crept round his neck and she buried her fingers in the thick hair, encountering its rough crispness with a tingle of sensual pleasure; melting to the strong beat of his heart against her own.

The sound of the door slamming and a female voice calling his name broke the spell and Philippa sprang up as Angela Stone walked into the room, her arms filled by a large brown paper parcel. For a moment the older woman looked startled, then she began to apologise: 'Oh dear, I'm sorry, Brent. I'd no idea you had a visitor.'

He smiled and held out his hand welcomingly. 'It's perfectly all right. I invited Philippa for coffee and sandwiches after the practice meeting. I dare say you'd like some too.'

Angela shook her head. 'I wouldn't dream of intruding. I just dropped by to bring you the curtains I took to the cleaner's for you.' She dropped the large parcel on to the settee, smiling at Philippa. 'And now if you'll excuse me, my dears, I'll be running along.'

'Oh, please don't go because of me!' Philippa bit her lip, realising that she sounded a little too eager – almost desperate. She shot a glance at Brent to see if he had noticed, but he looked unruffled. She took a deep breath and added: 'I'm sure you'd love a coffee, Miss Stone.'

Brent reiterated his offer. 'Of course you would. I'll just top up the pot.'

Angela began to pull off her gloves and hat, looking pleased. 'Well, as you're both so sure I'm not intruding, maybe I will have just one cup with you. Those stairs are terrible – I'm sure they add a few every time my back is turned!' She sat down on the settee with a sigh and Brent gave Philippa the ghost of a wink over her head as he went off to the kitchen to refill the coffee pot.

Philippa was grateful for the respite. Everything was moving too fast – before she had really had time to ask herself if this was what she wanted. If Brent was sincere in wanting to know her better she should be frank with him – tell him about the responsibility she had taken on – about Simon. After all, she wasn't exactly free in the full sense of the word.

'I'm glad we've met again like this,' Angela Stone was saying. 'I didn't get a chance to talk to you properly at the dance. Tell me, dear, how are you liking it here in Castle-bridge?'

'I'm settling down very well, thank you.'

'I hope you're meeting some nice young people of your own age. It can be so difficult to make friends when you work such unsocial working hours,' Angela went on. 'I'm always telling Brent he should find a nice girl and get married, but of course it isn't easy to meet the right young women when one is always working.' She adjusted a cushion comfortably into the small of her back. 'My friend Freda Standish has just come back from a world cruise with her niece, Emma.' She sighed. 'Now there's a dear girl. Freda and I had great hopes that something might materialise there. They made such a charming couple – but there, one can't force these things, can one? I think they must have had a tiff or something.' She sighed. 'Still, one can always hope.' She looked at Philippa. 'So many of you girls are career-orientated nowadays, but Emma isn't like that. That was why I thought her so suitable for Brent. She would have made an ideal doctor's wife. Since she's come home I've noticed a change in her, though. I saw her just this morning and she was bubbling over with the news that she'd just landed herself a job, and with my sister of all people!'

Philippa looked up. 'Your sister? That would be...'

Angela smiled. 'That's right, Brent's mother. She's been looking for a new secretary for some time and Emma did take a secretarial course after leaving school. Maybe it'll be good for her to have something interesting to occupy her.'

Brent came back into the room with the freshly brewed coffee and an extra cup, smiling at Philippa over his aunt's head. 'Now, are you currently taking sugar?' he asked as he poured. 'Or are you on one of your diets?'

'I usually have one of those little sweeteners, dear, but just this once I'll have sugar – just a *pinch*, mind.' She smiled at Philippa. 'Have to watch the inches so carefully when you get to my age. You know what they say – eat it today, wear it tomorrow!' She prattled on as she drank the coffee, telling Brent little snippets of news between sips.

The ringing of the telephone halted the conversation abruptly. Brent smiled apologetically as he got up to answer it. 'I've a feeling that might be Tag ringing from the GP Unit of Castlebridge District Hospital. We have a patient due any day who's threatening a breech presentation.' He rose, pushing a hand through his hair, and crossed the room to the telephone. 'Doctor Charlesworth.' Philippa heard a female voice speaking rapidly at the other end of the line, and after a moment he said briskly: 'Right, I'll be there as soon as I can, Sister.' He turned to Philippa, a rueful smile on his face. 'It's as I thought – there are threatened complications. I think I'd better get over there just in case.'

Angela Stone put down her cup and got to her feet. 'I'll be off, then.' She smiled at Philippa. 'Nice to have met you again, my dear. You must get Brent to bring you round for tea some Sunday afternoon. He knows he's always welcome to bring his friends.'

The three of them went downstairs together and Brent saw his aunt safely into her car. Turning to Philippa, he held out his hand. 'Come on, I'll take you to pick up your car.'

A few minutes later, as she made to get out of the car in the almost deserted car park of the Boar's Head, Brent reached for her, drawing her into his arms and kissing her briefly.

As she looked up at him, he gave her a wistful smile, brushing her chin playfully with his knuckles. 'Sorry the evening ended like this, but I dare say you're used to this kind of thing. Will you be all right?'

Philippa nodded. 'Of course. I hope all goes well at the hospital.'

Sitting in her own car, she watched as the Porsche swiftly turned and sped on its way towards the hospital. As she drove herself home she thought about Angela Stone's words. It was quite clear that she would like to see Brent and Emma married – that she thought them eminently suitable for each other. From what she said they had been close enough for it to have been on the cards too. She wondered what could have happened to break up the relationship. Had Brent really been in love with Emma, and had he turned to her – Philippa – on the rebound?

When she walked into the living room Dorcas rolled her eyes knowingly. 'Well, that must have been some meeting!'

Philippa looked at her watch and was shocked to see that it was almost eleven o'clock. Dismayed, she stared at Dorcas. 'Oh, good heavens! I'm sorry, Dorcas. What must you have thought of me?'

Dorcas grinned. 'I wouldn't like to tell you all the possibilities that have flitted through my mind!' she said with a twinkle. 'All I hope is that some of them are true! Surely a meeting that started at seven can't have gone on all this time?'

Philippa sank into a chair. 'No, it didn't.

Brent asked me to go for a drink afterwards. We finished up at his flat.'

'Wow! The plot thickens,' Dorcas said gleefully. 'But don't let me interrupt you. Go on.'

'There's nothing to tell. His aunt arrived with some curtains and as we were all having coffee together Brent was called out to a patient at the GP Unit.'

'Oh, bad luck. Still, if you will fall for a doctor...'

'Who said I'd fallen for him?' challenged Philippa.

'I did! Not a bit of good denying it. Only got to look at your eyes, like – what's the phrase they put in the books – *misty violets?*' laughed Dorcas. 'Or should that be two underdone poached eggs?'

Brought down to earth, Philippa laughed and threw a cushion at her friend. 'Trust you to knock all the romance out of it! Has Simon been all right?' she asked. 'Poor little boy. I've hardly spent any time at all with him this week.'

Dorcas smiled. 'He's fine, no need to worry. He's still on about that dog, though.'

'Oh dear,' sighed Philippa. 'I've tried to explain to him that it wouldn't be fair to leave a dog alone all day.'

'I did have one idea,' Dorcas said thoughtfully. 'The caretaker at school is looking for good homes for some motherless kittens. They're rather sweet, and he says they'll probably have to be put down if no one will take them.'

Philippa looked up at her. 'How would you feel about sharing your home with an animal?'

The other girl laughed. 'Couldn't be worse than my ex-husband! Shall we put it to Simon and see what he thinks about the compromise? When you come along to the parents' evening tomorrow we could take him to choose one.'

Friday was Philippa's half day off, and after lunch she took herself into town and had her hair done, then looked round the shops. Dorcas had been right about her wardrobe; it was sadly run down and out of date. It was time she did something about it. In the town's largest department store she bought two new dresses and a smart winter coat, all badly needed. Then, on her way out through the separates department, her attention was taken by a pair of cream cord jeans and a selection of attractive designer sweaters. She tried on the jeans and found they fitted perfectly, then chose a soft mohair sweater in a flattering shade of fuchsia pink to wear with them. She came home feeling light-hearted and happy. Maybe she hadn't quite said goodbye to her youth after all!

It was Philippa's first school parents' day, and she was fascinated at the way things had changed since she herself had been at school. She met Jane Fryer, Simon's teacher, and Simon proudly showed her his books and pointed to his various works of art, pinned up on the wall of the classroom. She was introduced to the rabbits and the hamster she had heard so much about, then, taking her hand, Simon announced that he was taking her to see the Safety First exhibition promoted and organised by Dorcas in the main hall. It was while they were looking at the exhibits that a voice spoke behind them:

'Good evening – it's Nurse James, isn't it?'

Philippa turned to see Emma Francis smiling at her. 'Hello. Are you enjoying it all?' Vaguely she wondered why Emma was here, then she recalled Dorcas telling her that Emma's father was on the board of school governors.

'It's quite a good school, isn't it?' Emma remarked conversationally. As she spoke she was looking curiously at Philippa; clearly she was also trying to work out the reason for her presence at the school open evening. There was an awkward silence as they regarded each other, broken by Simon as he tugged at Philippa's sleeve. 'Look, that's my safety first poster – there!' He pointed excitedly at a brightly coloured poster in the infants' section. On the bottom his name was printed in large proud capitals.

Emma's eyes followed the small pointing finger, and she leaned closer to get a better look. Ruffling his hair, she said: 'Is that really yours? It's *very* good. Who is that crossing the road so carefully?' She smiled encouragingly at him, and Simon turned suddenly shy and felt for Philippa's hand, glancing up at her uncertainly. Philippa gave his hand a reassuring squeeze.

'It looks like Samantha and her mummy to me,' she said quickly. 'And I'm sure that's you with them, helping them over the zebra crossing, isn't it?'

Simon nodded, but when Philippa glanced at Emma she saw that the other girl's face was looking vaguely puzzled, looking at the poster, then back at Simon.

Dorcas joined them. 'Well, what do you think of it? Some good work, eh?' She glanced at Emma. 'Hello, Emma. Enjoy your cruise?'

The other girl shrugged. 'It was all right, I suppose, though being shut up in a cruise ship with Aunt Freda for weeks at a time can get rather claustrophobic, if you know what I mean! I must say it's good to be home again.' She smiled. 'Well, I suppose I'd better go and see if I can find Daddy.'

When she had gone Dorcas looked at Philippa enquiringly. 'I saw her talking to you. What was she saying?'

Philippa lifted her shoulders. 'Nothing much.' She glanced down at Simon. 'She seems to be trying to take an interest in the school.'

Dorcas shrugged and took Simon's hand. 'I've got something to show you. I think Pippa's seen everything here now. I want you both to come along to Mr Smith's office.'

Dan Smith, the elderly school caretaker, had been warned of their visit, and he opened the door of his little cubbyhole with a smile. 'Come on in.' He looked down at the little boy. 'Now, let's see – it's Simon, isn't it? Come over here to the radiator and have a look in this box.'

Simon advanced cautiously and peeped

into the box where four chubby kittens snuggled warmly on a blanket, looking like a furry puzzle of paws, tails and noses. His face broke into a delighted smile and he turned to Philippa. 'Oh, Pippa, come and see! There are two black and white ones and two with brown on as well.'

The girls joined him and Philippa looked at Dorcas. 'Aren't they sweet?' She put a hand on Simon's shoulder. 'Would you like one, Simon? Cats can take care of themselves better than dogs. They're more suitable pets for people who have to be out a lot.'

'Now, if you were to take two they'd be company for each other,' the caretaker said craftily. He put a large hand on Simon's shoulder. 'You see, these poor little kittens haven't got a mother – she got run over. *You'd* have to be their mum.' The girls looked at each other as Simon stared wide-eyed at the caretaker and then back into the box, reaching in to touch one small silky head with a fingertip. The kitten opened large blue eyes and looked up at him, yawning to reveal a pink mouth and delicately curling tongue. 'Oh, *look*, he's smiling at me! I must have that one,' Simon said. 'Him and the one with the brown tip to his tail.' He looked up appealingly at them. 'Can I – *please?*'

Dorcas and Philippa looked at each other. Dan Smith had quite unashamedly conned them and they knew it. But one look at Simon's pleading eyes was enough to tell them it was in a good cause.

'They really are less trouble in pairs,' Dan assured them as he rummaged in the cupboard for a strong box in which to transport their new acquisitions. 'Amuse one another, they do, and don't tend to stray so much.' He seemed very knowledgeable about cats and instructed them in feeding and training, and ten minutes later Simon was sitting on the back seat of the car, carefully nursing the box and excitedly suggesting names for his new pets. Finally they agreed on Tippy, the one with the brown tip to his tail, and Smudge, who had a white face with a black smudge on his nose.

In all the excitement of settling them in – finding just the right place for their bed, two small feeding bowls and a strategically placed litter tray, Philippa had almost forgotten her meeting with Emma Francis. It was only after she was in bed some hours later that she remembered it. Emma really was extremely attractive. Her flawless complexion and smooth blonde hair made Philippa feel positively plain, yet there was an air of vulnerability about the girl that suggested that she didn't get all her own way in life. Once again Philippa found herself wondering just how close she and Brent had been – and what had happened to split them up. But it had been a long day, and she fell asleep in the middle of her speculations.

CHAPTER SEVEN

The first of the counselling clinics was to take place on the following Wednesday, and Doctor Frazer had warned them to expect it to be rather sparse. Clearly people would be diffident at first about coming along to talk out their problems. Perhaps their first 'customers' would be the most desperate cases, he speculated. Only time would tell.

Brent had been on call all weekend, so Philippa hadn't seen him. Monday was his day off and all day she had expected a call from him. By the time evening surgery was over she had resigned herself to the fact that he wasn't going to ring her. Perhaps he was busy at the flat, catching up on his paperwork, she told herself disappointedly.

As she was driving home that evening she passed the end of Heather Road and, on a sudden impulse, she turned the car into it and stopped at number five to see Mrs Haytor as she had promised. She found the old lady sitting happily in front of her large colour TV, a tea trolley drawn up to her armchair. She seemed pleased to see her visitor.

'I don't get many callers,' she told Philippa as she poured her a cup of tea. 'Only the nurse and that young lad with the ginger hair.' She shook her head. 'Calls himself a social worker, but if you ask me he's still wet behind the ears! Last time he came he yelled at me as though I was an idiot. "I might be a bit deaf," I told him, "but I'm not *daft!*"'

Philippa chuckled. 'And you're managing all right, are you?' she asked.

'Course I am,' the old lady assured her. 'I can see enough to get by, and since I've treated myself to this big new telly I can see that too.' She leaned forward conspiratorially. 'Mind you, I wouldn't tell *that* lot if I couldn't manage! When I go I want it to be in my own home. That's what I told Maureen, my daughter. I couldn't have stuck it down there with them for long.' She pulled down the corners of her mouth. 'She wanted to rule my life. Very bossy, my Maureen. Takes after her dad – always did. Then there was Reg, her husband. Resentment written all over him while I was there.' She shook her head. 'No, it would never have worked.'

Philippa looked around the neat, spotless room with its treasured knick-knacks, faded photographs and china ornaments, and knew instinctively that the old lady was right. She remembered all too well how Laura had blossomed once she was allowed to go home again among her own things, also how important it was for her to be allowed to do as much as she could for herself. 'Well, you can always talk to me,' she promised. 'I'm only the practice nurse and I'm visiting you simply as a friend, so if you have any problems just let me know. You can be sure I won't do anything to have you bundled into a home before you're ready to go.'

On Tuesday morning she was at the Centre early, arriving even before Jenny. She was looking through the mail in Reception when Doctor Frazer arrived.

'Good morning, Philippa.'

'Morning, Doctor.' She was continuing to sort through the mail when suddenly she realised that he was looking at her thoughtfully. She looked up. 'Is there anything wrong, Doctor?'

He took a deep breath. 'If you've got a moment to spare, I'd like you to come into my room for a chat,' he said.

Putting down the letters, Philippa followed apprehensively. What could he possibly want to talk to her about? As far as she knew her work was satisfactory.

In the surgery he closed the door and took off his coat. 'Do have a seat, Philippa,' he invited as he hung it up meticulously. He seated himself opposite her desk. Fixing her with a solicitous smile, he asked, 'Are you happy here with us?'

She moistened her dry lips. 'Yes – very. Why, is something wrong?'

'Not with your work,' he assured her. 'We've been lucky to find anyone to fit in with us so well.' He put the tips of his fingers together and regarded them thoughtfully. Obviously he was finding it difficult to find the words for whatever it was he wanted to say. 'I'd like to think that if you had a problem you'd feel that you could come to us with it, Philippa,' he said at last. 'I don't want to pry. The last thing we do here is intrude into our employees' personal lives. But if you need a spot of fatherly advice at any time, quite confidentially, of course...' he cleared his throat. 'I have daughters of about your age, so you needn't feel shy. They're both married now, but they had their share of romantic entanglements, I can tell you.'

He laughed awkwardly, and suddenly light dawned. He was talking about her developing relationship with Brent! He must have heard that they had been out together a few times. A thought struck her: perhaps he didn't approve. Might it be that he was trying to warn her of something? she smiled tentatively. 'Do you disapprove, Doctor?'

He looked startled. 'Oh, good heavens, no! It's not for me to make judgements of that kind. As long as everything works out for you and you're happy...'

'I am,' she told him. 'Coming here was the best move I could have made, and I feel that I can make a new start just as long as I don't rush things...' She took a deep breath – he seemed so keen for her to confide in him; so much so that she felt obliged to tell him something about her past. 'There was someone before, you see – when I had to give up my training it ended. I was hurt at the time. It makes one wary.'

He nodded sympathetically. 'Of course, my dear, I quite understand. There's no need to go into details. As I said before, I don't mean to pry. I just wanted you to know that we are your friends – we're here if you need us at any time.'

'Of course – thank you.' Philippa stood up, feeling slightly embarrassed. What could have brought on this sudden rush of concern? she wondered. She looked at her watch. 'Oh dear, just look at the time! I'd better get along to my room and change into my uniform before the rush starts.'

She worked her way through the morning's surgery, bandaging, changing dressings, taking blood tests and labelling them ready for their trip to the local path lab. Sometimes the work was very routine and she longed for something more responsible, more demanding. But when these thoughts occurred to her she usually pushed them firmly to the back of her mind. She was lucky to have found such a convenient job. She should be thankful.

She had seen the last patient and was almost ready to start clearing up when there was a tentative tap on the door. She looked up in surprise and called: 'Come in!'

The door opened and Gladys slipped into the room. 'Can I have a word, Nurse?' she asked.

'Of course, Gladys. Sit down.' Philippa looked at the cleaner with concern. She was unusually subdued this morning and she looked as though she'd slept badly. There were dark circles under her eyes and she hadn't taken the usual trouble with her make-up. Clearly there was something troubling her. 'Now, what can I do for you?' asked Philippa with what she hoped was an encouraging smile.

Gladys sat on the edge of the chair and twisted her fingers nervously in her lap. 'I don't really know where to begin,' she muttered.

Philippa waited, not wanting to hurry her over something she was obviously having difficulty in expressing. At last, watching the woman's discomfort for a moment, she asked gently: 'Aren't you well? Is there something you want to ask?'

Gladys took a deep breath and looked up. 'I don't know – it may be nothing.' She frowned and looked down at her hands.

Philippa waited a moment, then asked gently: 'What may be nothing, Gladys?'

'I've been putting it off – hoping it would go away...' Gladys spoke quietly, almost as though to herself. 'It's Shane I worry about, you see; he's only got me since his dad left us ten years ago. He's just coming up to fifteen. It's a difficult age. He really needs a father and I don't know what'd become of him if he didn't have me either!'

Philippa could see that there was something quite serious on the woman's mind. Now that she had made up her mind to talk to someone about it it was as though the floodgates had opened. As she continued her words came faster and faster until she was almost incoherent. Philippa got up and came round to sit closer to her on the corner of the desk. 'Gladys…' she interrupted gently, 'I don't understand. What makes you think that Shane might have to be without you? Will you tell me what it is that's troubling you? Maybe it's something I can help with.'

Gladys stopped in mid-sentence. 'It's this lump,' she said, suddenly coming to the point. One hand went involuntarily to her left breast. 'It was such a shock when I found it. I've always been so healthy.'

Philippa nodded. She had suspected something of the kind. It explained Gladys's reaction to the counselling clinic and her fierce determination to keep her troubles to herself. She had seen it so many times before. She smiled sympathetically. 'Tell me a little about it. How long ago was it when you first discovered it?'

Gladys drew in her breath. It was obviously an enormous relief to have the problem out in the open. 'About six months ago,' she said with a sigh. 'I've tried not to think about it, but lately I haven't been able to sleep for worrying.' She turned a stricken face up to

Philippa. 'It isn't *me* I'm bothered about. It's Shane. A while ago he got in with a rough crowd and I keep having nightmares about what might happen to him if I wasn't there.'

Philippa laid her hand on the woman's trembling arm. 'I think you *should* think of yourself before you start worrying about anything else. To begin with, will you let me have a look? And will you take my advice if I give it?'

Gladys nodded eagerly. 'Oh yes. I can't take any more worry. Whatever it is I'd rather know.'

Philippa made a brief examination and found a small hard mass about the size of a walnut. She smiled reassuringly. 'I'd like you to see the doctor with this, Gladys – not because I think you have anything to worry about, but because you'll need treatment for it that I'm not qualified to give you.'

Gladys swallowed hard and asked, 'What do you think it is? Is it...' she broke off, unable to frame the word.

Philippa shook her head. 'I can tell you that thousands of women get something of this sort at some time in their lives and I'm ninety per cent sure that what you have is nothing worse than a simple benign cyst, but naturally it's better to be sure, otherwise

151

you'll still worry, won't you?'

Gladys nodded, licking dry lips. 'What will they do? Does it mean an operation?' she asked.

'Not nowadays,' Philippa told her. 'At least not if my diagnosis is correct. The doctor will most probably send you to the hospital to see a consultant. He'll draw off the fluid from the cyst and send it for analysis; that will tell him whether it's likely to be troublesome.'

'And then?'

'Then you can stop worrying. If it's harmless there's nothing more to be done – and please believe me when I tell you that a very small percentage of these little lumps turn out to be anything sinister, and even in the unlikely event of its being serious, there's a very good chance of a complete cure. You're far more likely to be harmed by worrying about it.'

Gladys went off to get dressed, looking relieved, and by the time she came back Philippa had rung through to Jenny and made an appointment for her to see Brent next morning. She wrote the time on a slip of paper and handed it to Gladys. 'You won't forget to keep the appointment, will you?'

The cleaner smiled tremulously. 'If I did have to go into hospital, what about Shane?'

Philippa shook her head. 'You must try not to worry so much about him. He's almost fifteen, as you say. He's not a baby any more. You must think about yourself a little more.'

Gladys coloured. 'You don't know what it is to be a mother,' she said. 'Specially one with no husband! I couldn't expect you to understand. You never stop feeling responsible for them, you know.'

Philippa smiled. 'I dare say you're right. But suppose we cross that bridge when we come to it?'

When Gladys had gone she sat at her desk for a long moment, deep in thought. What Gladys had said was right. When one took on the responsibility of parenthood it was for life – and anyone sharing that life would have to share the responsibility. Peter hadn't been prepared to do it; was it fair to expect any man to?

Philippa had done her best to create an informal atmosphere for the first of the counselling clinics, staying on after evening surgery ended to tidy the waiting room where it was to be held; arranging the chairs in a less formal pattern and preparing coffee and biscuits. She had even bought some chrysanthemums on her way to the Health Centre that morning and made a cheerful arrangement as a centrepiece for the table.

It had been decided that three counsellors should be on duty; herself, Nick Cornish and Brent, who arrived just as she was running a comb through her hair in the office. She saw the door open through the mirror and her heart gave the now familiar leap at the sight of his tall figure entering the room. She turned with a smile. 'Hello. I think everything is ready.'

He put his case down on Jenny's desk. 'Good.' He glanced at her and the smile froze on her face at the coldness in his eyes.

'I've hardly seen you this week,' she said, feeling suddenly nervous and awkward.

'I dare say we've both been busy.' He didn't look at her as he thumbed through the message pad on the desk.

Philippa gave a nervous little laugh. 'If you're looking for messages, I don't think there are any – for once. I looked through a moment ago to see if you'd have a clear run for the clinic this evening.'

Brent closed the pad and straightened up. He looked tired and there were lines of strain around his mouth as he said, 'I've been at the hospital most of the afternoon. Helen Hunter was rushed in just before lunch.'

Philippa caught her breath. 'Oh – not...?'

His face told her the answer even before he spoke. 'Yes. We did everything possible, but she lost the baby about an hour ago.'

'Oh, Brent, I'm sorry.' She went to him and laid a hand on his arm, but when he returned her gaze the look in his eyes made her flinch. She took an involuntary step backwards. 'Brent! It's not just Helen, is it? What's wrong?'

'Why couldn't you have trusted me?' he demanded, his voice dangerously low and controlled. He took a step towards her and grasped her wrist, his eyes blazing into hers, as green as a stormy sea. 'Why didn't you tell me?'

Philippa shook her head uncomprehendingly, her eyes wide with astonishment. 'I – haven't the least idea what you...'

'Evening, all!' The door opened to admit Nick. He wore his usual cheery grin, which faded as he stood in the doorway absorbing the tense atmosphere in the office. As Philippa and Brent moved away from one another he said heartily: 'Well, it's a fine

155

evening. Good omen for the first clinic, eh?'
He looked from one to the other and added:
'Oh dear, am I butting in on something
again? Sorry.'

Brent turned the full force of his blazing
eyes on him. 'As a psychologist, Cornish,
you'd make a damned good greengrocer!'
He pushed angrily past the amazed social
worker, slamming the door behind him.

Nick stared at Philippa, his face comically
taken aback as he spread his hands. 'Well!
Pardon me for living!' He appealed to her.
'What did I *say*, for God's sake?'

Philippa shrugged. 'He's had a bad day
that's all.'

Nick took a step towards her, peering into
her face enquiringly. 'You don't look too
clever yourself. Want to tell Uncle Nick all
about it? Lovers' tiff, was it?'

Philippa picked up her bag and walked
past him. 'Grow up, Nick,' she told him
shortly.

By half past eight only two people had
arrived. Philippa recognised them from the
odd occasions when she had assisted Brent
at the ante-natal clinic. They were Sandra
Brown and her mother Doreen. Sandra
looked bored as she sat awkwardly in her
chair, eating biscuits from the plate on the

table. Her mother looked at Philippa apologetically.

'Never stops eating,' she whispered, nudging her daughter at the same time. Sandra shifted her position and frowned sulkily. 'Well, eatin' for two, aren't I?'

Brent looked at his watch and cleared his throat. 'Well, I think we may as well start.' He smiled at Mrs Brown. 'It seems you have the floor to yourselves, Mrs Brown. How can we help you?'

'Just tell her it's not on – her keeping the baby,' she demanded. 'She won't listen to me – thinks it's all sweet little cherubs in frilly cradles, she does. I've tried to tell her. I can see what it'll be: *me* left holding the baby when she gets sick of sleepless nights and dirty nappies. She'll meet some bloke and go off and get married and I'll…'

Brent held up a hand. 'Mrs Brown, wait a minute! Can we take one point at a time? May we hear what Sandra thinks?' He looked at the girl. 'Have you really thought it through, Sandra? After all, you won't receive any support from the baby's father, will you?'

She shrugged apathetically, taking another biscuit from the rapidly diminishing pile on the plate. 'There's always the Social.'

'It would be an awful struggle, bringing a baby up on your own and trying to live on Social Security, Sandra,' Philippa put in. 'And if your mother is going to have to help support you both, don't you think you should discuss it together – try to agree on some kind of compromise?'

The girl shrugged unco-operatively. 'Dunno.'

Nick cleared his throat. 'I think that if Sandra wants to keep her baby and try to make a go of it on her own she should be encouraged,' he said. 'We could put her name down for a flat.'

Mrs Brown looked appalled. 'She's only sixteen! She was at school this time last year. She isn't capable of looking after herself, let alone living alone and coping with a baby!'

Nick smiled confidently. 'Perhaps you underestimate your daughter.'

Sandra grinned cheekily at her mother. 'Yeah, pr'aps you do that!'

Philippa looked at the couple and knew that she was looking at a recipe for disaster. Sandra, she knew, was due to have her baby in a few weeks' time. What was really behind her decision to keep the child? she wondered. Did she genuinely have a maternal instinct, or was it mere stubbornness towards her mother? She couldn't help thinking with irony of Helen Hunter, breaking her heart in her hospital bed this evening at the loss of yet another baby, while they sat here deciding the fate of Sandra's offspring; already resented even before it was born. Sometimes it seemed there was no justice in the world. Of the three of them only Nick seemed confident of the answer. He was all for letting Sandra have her own way. Already he was promising to look into the possibility of finding accommodation for her and her new baby, while her mother looked on helplessly. Suddenly Philippa had an idea.

'Sandra, how would you like to go along to the Council Day Nursery and give a hand a couple of days a week?' she suggested. 'They're always short of helpers, and that way you'd get an idea of what caring for a baby all day is like.' Sandra looked reluctant and she added encouragingly: 'You do like babies, don't you?'

The girl lifted her shoulders. 'Dunno really.'

'Well, this would certainly help you to find out.'

'I think that's an excellent idea,' Brent put in. 'If you like I'll ask our health visitor to call round and talk to you about it.'

When they had gone Nick hurried into his office, clearly not wishing to cross swords with Brent again. Philippa began to gather up the dirty cups, stacking them on the tray, her eyes avoiding Brent's.

'Well, you'd hardly call that a resounding success, would you?' he asked, his voice flat with depression.

She put the tray down and looked at him. 'We're still learning. I think we did our best,' she said. 'Perhaps it was just as well we didn't have a full house.'

He looked at her. 'That was a good idea of yours about the day nursery – if we can get her there. She looks bone idle to me.'

Philippa laughed. 'Nancy Marshall, the health visitor, will get her there if anyone can. I'll have a word with her.' She bit her lip, longing to get at the reason for this new inexplicable barrier between them. 'Brent, would you mind telling me what all that was about earlier? What did you mean when you asked why I didn't trust you?'

He rose to his feet and sighed deeply. 'I *know*, Philippa,' he told her. 'Why couldn't you have told me? Why were you so cagey? What reaction did you expect, for God's sake? Surely you know that I...' He broke off as footsteps were heard in the corridor outside. A moment later the door opened and Emma looked in. She smiled brightly when she saw them both, apparently unaware of the tension that hung in the air.

'Oh, good, you're still here.' She came into the room and closed the door, looking anxiously at Brent. 'I was talking to your Aunt Angela last night. Daddy and I had dinner with Doctor Frazer and his wife – your aunt was there too. She seemed worried about you – said she thought you were working too hard. She suggested that I come along and take you out for a meal.' She gave a little selfconscious laugh, glancing at Philippa. 'Actually, I've booked a table, so I hope you haven't arranged anything else.'

There was a silence as Emma looked from one to the other, then, sensing that the other girl wanted her out of the way, Philippa moved towards the door. 'Well, I'll be going, then, if there's nothing else – Doctor Charlesworth?'

He shot her a look of pure steel. 'No – as you say, there's nothing else, obviously. Goodnight, Nurse.' He turned his attention to Emma. 'How thoughtful of you to book a table. Now that you mention it I am hungry.

161

Shall we go?'

As they went out through the door together, Emma chattering excitedly, Philippa turned to see Nick Cornish watching from the doorway of his office. He raised an eyebrow at her. 'Phew!' he whistled. 'If *that's* the competition no wonder you look so down in the mouth!'

CHAPTER EIGHT

When Philippa came down to breakfast the following morning Dorcas was already halfway through her breakfast. She looked up as her friend came into the kitchen. 'Good lord, you look awful,' she said with characteristic candour. 'Did you sleep badly?'

'I was a bit restless – must have been something I ate.' Philippa had no wish to recall the long hours of the night, during which she had lain awake wondering what Brent had heard to make him so angry with her. She busied herself cutting bread for toast.

'I've done some scrambled eggs,' Dorcas waved a hand towards the cooker. 'Help yourself.'

As Philippa dished up the eggs Simon, who had been finishing his bowl of cereal at the table, jumped down and went to get milk from the fridge for the kittens. Dorcas grinned at Philippa over his head. Adopting them had certainly been a success, and he seemed to be taking to heart the caretaker's suggestion that he should be their 'mother', fussing over them, feeding and playing with them as often as he could.

Dorcas sat down and began to tuck into her breakfast. 'You haven't mentioned Doctor Charming Charlesworth lately,' she remarked, buttering a piece of toast. 'What's wrong? You haven't had a row, I hope.'

Philippa shook her head. 'It's been all go at the Health Centre lately,' she said evasively.

'Why don't you ask him round for a meal some time?' suggested Dorcas. 'I could always make myself scarce that evening. After all, you've been to his place.' When Philippa didn't reply she went on: 'I do want you to think of this as your home, you know, Pippa.'

'I – I'm afraid our relationship seems to have taken a backward step,' Philippa said awkwardly. 'Last night after the clinic he went out to dinner with Emma. She arrived to collect him, saying that she'd booked a table. It seems she'd been talking to Miss Stone. Brent's aunt seems determined to see him married – preferably to that young lady.'

Dorcas paused, her toast halfway to her mouth. 'Ah, so that's it! I knew there was something wrong.' She shook her head. 'Well, aren't you going to do anything about it?'

Philippa shrugged. 'What do you suggest?' she asked laconically.

Dorcas gave a snort. 'Well, you're not going to take it lying down, are you?'

Philippa looked up with a wry smile. 'It's entirely up to Brent, the company he chooses, isn't it? He does have a mind of his own, you know – a strong one too. If he goes out with Emma it will be because he wants to. I don't see that there's anything I can do about it.'

'Oh, wake up, girl!' Dorcas said impatiently. 'Don't pretend you don't care, because I know differently. Look, if you think...' Suddenly her attention was diverted by Simon coughing. 'Hello, young man. I hope you're not getting a cold,' she said, looking over at him as he played with the kittens. She shook her head at Philippa. 'The school is full of them at the moment. It's always the same at this time of year.' She got up from the table and began to clear her dishes on to the draining board. 'Ah well, soon be half-term.'

Philippa looked at her watch. 'I'll give you a hand with the washing-up, then I must fly.'

As soon as she arrived at the Health Centre and walked into Reception she heard the roar of the vacuum cleaner as Gladys went about her daily chores. Philippa found her putting the final touches to Doctor Frazer's room. Popping her head round the door, she greeted her: 'Morning, Gladys. You haven't forgotten you have an appointment at nine, have you?'

Gladys switched off the vacuum cleaner and nodded. 'Don't need any reminding about that. Can't say I'm exactly looking forward to it, I can tell you.'

Philippa patted her shoulder. 'Well, if it's any comfort, I'll be there. It's part of my job to assist at that kind of examination! It won't be too bad, I promise.'

Gladys smiled. 'It's a relief to know it's out of my hands,' she confided.

Philippa was just leaving the room when the cleaner spoke again: 'Nurse, I want to apologise for something I said to you yesterday.'

Philippa looked round in surprise. 'Something you said? What was that?'

'About you not knowing what it was like to be a parent.' Gladys chewed her lip, her eyes sliding away from Philippa's. 'I've – *heard* since then, you see.'

Frowning, Philippa turned and came back into the room, pushing the door to behind her. 'How do you mean? What have you heard, Gladys?'

The cleaner looked embarrassed. 'About – well, you know – about your little boy. *I* say it's all to your credit. After all, you could have given him up for adoption, couldn't you? Giving up training to be a doctor to keep him couldn't have been easy.' She glanced at Philippa uneasily. 'Well, that's it. I just wanted you to know that I'm on your side, that's all.'

Philippa was staring at her incredulously. So many things suddenly becoming clear: the talk Doctor Frazer had had with her yesterday morning that she had found so puzzling. She had totally misunderstood that! Brent's anger and his reference to 'lack of trust' had obviously been based on the same assumption. But where had this piece of gossip come from, and who had been spreading it? Suddenly like a bolt from the blue came the answer. In her mind's eye she saw herself and Simon looking at the posters at the school's open evening; Simon's name, printed in large capitals on the bottom of his exhibit – the same name as hers; Emma's large blue eyes as she had looked from one to the other of them, obviously putting two and two together and coming to the obvious conclusion! Finally something she had said when she arrived at the Health Centre to pick Brent up; 'Daddy and I had dinner with Doctor Frazer and his wife last night.' She must have started the rumour then!

'I'm afraid you've been misinformed, Gladys,' she said quietly. 'Where did you hear this story?'

Scarlet-faced, the cleaner was just beginning to splutter out an incoherent answer when the door opened and Doctor Frazer came in.

'Ah, good morning, ladies,' he said cheerily.

Gladys quickly muttered an apology and escaped hastily with her vacuum cleaner. Philippa closed the door behind her. 'May I have a word with you, Doctor?'

He looked surprised. 'Of course. Sit down.' He looked at her enquiringly. 'Something troubling you?'

Philippa took a deep breath. 'Quite by chance, I've just heard the gossip that's being put around,' she told him. 'I believe it must be what you were referring to yesterday. I think I ought to set the record straight. Simon James, the six-year-old I'm bringing up, is my nephew. He was my brother's child. His father was killed in an accident two years ago and his mother died shortly before we moved here. She was the invalid I gave up my training to nurse.'

Doctor Frazer looked acutely embarrassed. 'Oh, my dear, I'm so sorry. But why didn't you tell us these facts when you came for your interview? It would have saved us all a lot of embarrassment.'

'I didn't want you to think I was trying to play on your sympathy,' Philippa explained. 'Coming to Castlebridge was meant to be a new start for Simon and me. I wanted to put the past behind us.'

'I see.' He shook his head sadly. 'I'm afraid we can never quite do that, my dear,' he said. 'The past often has a nasty habit of catching up with one in unexpected ways. Better to be forearmed.' He smiled. 'Do accept my sincere apologies, Philippa, and please believe me when I tell you that I spoke only out of concern for you.'

'Of course.' Philippa got up and went to the door, hesitating as she reached it. 'I wonder if you'd do something for me, Doctor?'

'Of course, anything I can.'

'Will you tell the truth to anyone else who's heard this rumour – here at the Centre, I mean? It would be rather awkward for me to do it myself.'

He smiled warmly, getting up from his desk and coming across to take her hand. 'I shall be only too happy to do that. And once again, I'm sorry for jumping to the wrong conclusion.'

Just after nine Philippa was called to Brent's surgery to assist with Gladys's examination. The cleaner was obviously nervous as she scanned the faces of both doctor and nurse, tuned to pick up the slightest anxiety either of them might betray. But Brent calmly confirmed what Philippa had already told her. After Gladys had dressed and was seated once more at his desk he told her: 'I'm making you an appointment to see Mr Frobisher at Castlebridge District Hospital.' He gave her a quick, reassuring smile. 'This isn't because I'm anxious about this little lump of yours, it's just the routine procedure. It won't be a long wait, so there won't be too much time for you to worry about it.'

Gladys thanked him and left, looking relieved. Philippa glanced at Brent, who was writing on his pad. 'She confided to me yesterday that she's been worrying herself silly about this lump she'd discovered,' she told him. 'She's really much more worried about having to leave her son than about herself. I tried to reassure her and put her in the picture a little.' She looked at him. 'What would you say it is – a cyst?'

He straightened up and met her eyes impersonally. 'Probably, though one can never say for certain. You did right to get her to see me, though.'

Philippa hesitated, then took a deep breath and began: 'Brent...' But at that moment there was a tap on the door and Jenny looked in, a sheaf of papers in her hand.

'You asked for these notes, Doctor Charlesworth. I've been waiting for a gap so that I could bring them in.' She glanced at Philippa. 'There are some patients waiting for dressings, Nurse. I said you wouldn't be long.'

'Of course – I'm coming now.' Philippa glanced at Brent, but his head was once more bent, this time over the notes Jenny had brought him. This was neither the time nor the place to have a personal discussion. She should have known better. Turning, she hurried back to her own room.

For once it was a fairly quiet surgery as far as Philippa was concerned. Now that the

171

children were back at school there were fewer minor injuries to attend to. At ten o'clock she glanced at her watch and began to tidy her room, looking forward to a much needed cup of coffee and a chat with Jenny. As she checked her equipment she wondered how many of the staff Doctor Frazer had got around to talking to. He hadn't had a lot of time. She would probably find herself having to put some people straight herself after all. He had been right, she told herself. She really should have made her position clear right at the outset as Dorcas had advised. Oddly enough, this particular complication had never even occurred to her.

She took a last look around the room and was just about to go out into Reception when the door opened and Brent came in. He stood with his back to the closed door and for a moment they looked at each other, neither of them speaking. Philippa's heart began to pound uneasily. If he had come to apologise… She opened her mouth to speak, but he beat her to it.

'Greg has just told me,' he said, 'about your small nephew. For God's sake, Philippa, why didn't you tell me in the first place? And why didn't you say something yesterday?'

She swallowed hard, her heart beating fast. Although the mistake was his, he was obviously still putting the onus on her. 'Because I hadn't the vaguest idea at the time what you were talking about,' she told him shakily. Even to herself, her voice sounded wavery and close to tears. 'You spoke of trust. It seems to me that you were rather lacking in that particular virtue yourself! Evidently you were ready to believe anything you heard about me without even giving me the benefit of the doubt!'

Brent frowned. 'I'm not making excuses for myself. You're right, of course,' he said stiffly. 'But you must admit that your silence – your air of secrecy...'

'My air of *secrecy?*' Philippa interrupted sharply. 'I came here to apply for a job, not to protest my innocence! My domestic situation had nothing to do with it.'

He took a step towards her. 'It has a lot to do with me, though. I'd flattered myself that I was more than just your employer!' His hands shot out to grasp her shoulders. 'I thought we were – friends, Philippa; very good friends. I've already told you that I have a deep admiration for you. Didn't that mean anything at all to you?' He looked into her eyes and she felt her hurt and resentment beginning to recede under their clear blue gaze. At the corner of his mouth a tiny pulse throbbed as he shook her gently. 'Well, didn't it?' he asked. He drew her towards him, but she stiffened, holding back rigidly, pride refusing to allow her to back down so easily.

'It – isn't as simple as that, Brent,' she said painfully. 'My life isn't exactly mine to do as I like with any more. Whatever anyone might tell you, being responsible for another human being isn't to be taken lightly. It doesn't really make any difference that Simon isn't my own son. He's still with me to stay, and anyone who doesn't like the idea…'

'Who *said* they didn't like the idea?' he interrupted angrily, grasping her shoulders. 'It seems to me that you're taking an awful lot for granted, Philippa.'

She pulled away from him and walked across to the window, looking out on to the leaf-strewn car park. 'I learned a long time ago never to take *anything* for granted, Brent,' she told him quietly. 'I thought we were friends too. But I also got the distinct impression that there was more than friendship between you and Emma Francis.' She turned to look him straight in the eye.

'And I don't think I'd be taking too much for granted if I assumed it was she who told you about Simon?'

Flecks of green flashed angrily in the blue eyes, turning their warmth to ice. 'Emma did mention it, yes. I'm sure she didn't mean you any harm by doing so. She obviously thought it was common knowledge, as indeed it should have been!'

Philippa's nerves snapped. 'I've never tried to keep Simon a secret! But I was under the impression that my private life was my own affair.' She swallowed hard at the tears that tightened her throat.

He frowned, shaking his head. 'All right, if that's the way you want it!' He glared at her. 'It seems to me that you have a king-size chip on your shoulder. But as you've just made so abundantly clear – it's none of my business!' He turned and walked out of the room, slamming the door behind him.

Philippa stood where she was, staring at the closed door, tears pricking her eyelids and her throat tight with angry frustration. She clenched her hands into tight fists. Damn! What the devil had got into her to make her so stubborn and awkward? In his own way he had been trying to apologise and she had thrown his apology back in his

175

teeth; sent him away when he was the one person she longed to turn to. 'Driven him straight into Emma's arms,' was the way Dorcas would probably have put it! Now whatever had been about to blossom between them was over, and she had only herself to blame.

Her knees were trembling so much that she was obliged to sit down at her desk again. She decided to wait until the three doctors had left for their rounds before she showed her face in the office. With a heavy heart she thought about her position here. Could she stay on now? Surely the situation would be intolerable – working with Brent and trying to pretend that nothing had happened? She had inadvertently ruined the good beginning she had made at the Health Centre too.

It was ten minutes later when a tap on the door heralded Jenny, a steaming cup in her hand. 'You didn't come for your coffee, so I've brought it in.' She took one look at Philippa's face and came inside. Putting the cup down on the desk, she said: 'It's all right – I've heard. Gladys told me earlier that the story about you was wrong, then Doctor Frazer told us officially just now.' She pulled a face. 'I reckon you could sue whoever put it about.'

Philippa took a sip of her coffee and shrugged. 'It's hardly slander to say that I have a son,' she said flatly. 'It was a natural assumption to make, I suppose. It was my fault – I should have made it clear before. I just didn't see why anyone should be interested. Besides, Simon and I have had our fill of sympathy.'

Jenny sat down on the chair opposite. 'Poor little boy! He's lucky to have you. It can't be easy for either of you, I can see that. Does he ask about his mother?' she asked. 'What does he tell his friends at school?'

'That he lives with me, I suppose,' Philippa told her. 'He's never mentioned Laura to me since she died. That's why I thought moving away from where it all happened – making a new life...'

The other girl frowned. 'You can't really run away from problems, though, can you?' she said thoughtfully. 'You know the child best, of course, but I think if I were you I'd get him to talk about it – get it all out into the open. So that you know what's going on in his mind. Kids are funny.' She grinned. 'But I dare say it was to avoid advice like this that you kept it all quiet! Better tell me to mind my own business before I stick my neck out too far!' From the other end of the corridor the insistent ring of the telephone could be heard, and Jenny got to her feet with a sigh. 'I'd better go and answer that. Drink your coffee up before it gets cold.'

Philippa did as she was told, gratefully sipping the hot drink, glad of the comforting warmth of the cup between her hands. But Jenny had given her food for thought. Advising other people about their problems was one thing – solving your own was quite another matter.

That night as she put Simon to bed Philippa thought about Jenny's advice. As she tucked him up for the night she paused, wondering if this might be a good moment to have that talk with him, but the thought of it overwhelmed her. Suddenly she felt too weary, at a loss to know where to begin. She dropped a kiss on top of the curly head and put out the light, biting her lip as she made her way downstairs. 'You're a coward, Philippa James,' she reproached herself. 'Maybe you always have been where Simon is concerned.'

Dorcas was out. John Dixon had been asking to take her out to dinner for weeks and she had finally relented. Alone downstairs, Philippa sat watching TV for a while, then switched off and picked up a magazine. She must have dozed, tired from the previous night's restlessness. Suddenly she woke with a start and looked at her watch. It was half-past ten. Something must have woken her – she heard it again. Upstairs Simon was coughing wheezily, calling her name feebly.

She took the stairs two at a time and threw open his door, switching on the light. 'It's all right, darling, Pippa's here.' The little boy was sitting up in bed, gasping for breath, his face white, the lips tinged with blue. His appearance frightened her. She had seen children like this before in the paediatric ward of the hospital where she had trained – children having an asthma attack. But Simon didn't suffer from asthma!

Hurriedly she packed a chair with pillows and got him out of bed, propping him upright and opening the windows. She tried to calm him, but he was badly frightened by his inability to expel his breath – a fact which only exacerbated the attack. She tried frantically to think of other ways in which she might help him. If only she had some oxygen handy! For another agonising minute she watched him fighting, listening to the agonised rasping of his breath.

Suddenly she made up her mind. 'I'm going to get the doctor for you, darling. Don't worry, I'll be right back,' she told him.

In the hall she dialled Doctor Martin's number, wishing they had had a chance to meet and get to know the elderly doctor before something as traumatic as this happened. It was bad enough for Simon to be having the attack, without being treated by a doctor he didn't know. She heard the receiver being lifted at the other end and a woman's voice answered:

'Doctor Martin's housekeeper. Can I help you?'

Philippa explained the situation as briefly as she could, stressing the urgency. 'I know it's late, but I'd be very grateful if Doctor Martin could come and see him,' she finished.

'I'm sorry, Doctor Martin is ill,' the woman told her. 'But if you don't mind his locum...'

'No, of course not. As soon as possible, please.'

The woman took the address and promised that a doctor would be there in minutes. Philippa replaced the receiver with trembling fingers. Strange how different one felt when the patient was one's own flesh and blood.

For all her training and experience she felt as helpless and worried as a complete novice.

Back in the bedroom Simon's breathing was no easier, and he looked at her in mute appeal as she took his cold little hand. She could see that the muscles of his neck were becoming sucked in now, and it hurt her to watch the laboured heaving of his chest. She could see that he was near exhaustion and inwardly she prayed that the doctor wouldn't be long.

'Try not to worry, darling,' she said, feeling helpless and ineffectual. 'The doctor will be here very soon and he'll give you something to make you better.'

Doctor Martin's housekeeper was as good as her word. Although it seemed like hours, Philippa's watch told her that exactly ten minutes had elapsed since her telephone call when she heard a car draw up outside. The relief was almost overwhelming as she bent forward to kiss Simon's cheek. 'That'll be the doctor now. I'll go and let him in. I'll only be a minute.'

Running downstairs, she threw open the front door. 'Thank you for coming so promptly, Doctor. I– *Oh!*' She stopped, the words dying on her lips as she stared at the man standing on the threshold. A man she

181

hadn't seen for almost two years – someone she had not expected to see again ever, and certainly not here in Castlebridge.

For his part, Doctor Peter Gilbert looked equally surprised. 'Philippa! Good heavens, what on earth are you doing here?'

She swallowed hard. All she felt was relief – the relief one feels on encountering a familiar face in trouble. Just for the moment the fact that he was her ex-fiancé was irrelevant.

CHAPTER NINE

Peter made a brief but thorough examination of Simon. His calm manner and the fact that he was already known to the child helped.

'I haven't seen you for a long time,' he remarked cheerily as he took a phial out of his case and gave Simon an injection. 'You've grown a lot – I'd hardly have recognised you! I bet you even go to school now, eh?' He handed Philippa the disposable syringe and empty phial, then snapped his case shut and sat down on the edge of the bed to regard Simon with a smile. 'Now listen, old chap. I think we should pop along to the hospital. They've got something there that will stop all this nonsense and make you better in no time. Understand?'

Simon nodded, looking at Philippa for her approval.

'It'll probably only be for the night,' Peter went on. 'Then you'll be able to come home again – go back to school – right?' Simon was obviously reassured and nodded his understanding. Peter stood up and looked at Philippa. 'We won't bother with an ambulance, I'll take him in my car. May I use your telephone?'

'Of course. It's in the hall.' On the landing she pulled the door to behind her and looked at him enquiringly. 'This is the first time anything like this has happened. Obviously it's asthma – but why?'

He shrugged. 'Anyone's guess. I've given him a shot of Pethidine to relax the muscles. That'll ease his breathing a little, but we need to get some oxygen into him, then have another look in the morning. He's badly shocked at the moment, poor little chap. We'll be able to get a better picture after he's had a good night's sleep.' In the hall as he dialled the hospital's number he caught sight of the kittens in their box through the half-open kitchen door. Glancing at Philippa, he pointed to them. 'How long have you had those?'

'A few days.' She looked at him. 'Oh! You don't think...?'

But he was through to the hospital – making arrangements for Simon's admission.

After scribbling a hasty note for Dorcas, Philippa went with Simon to the hospital.

Sitting in the back, she held him, cocooned in a warm blanket and drowsy from the effects of the Pethidine. At the hospital he was taken out of her arms and she was told to wait. She looked at Peter appealingly. 'Can't I come up with him?'

He shook his head, putting a hand on her shoulder. 'Better for both of you this way. You'll be able to see him once he's settled.' His fingers tightened reassuringly. 'Don't worry, I'll take you home afterwards.'

'But – can't I stay with him?' she asked, her lip trembling.

Peter shook his head. 'Pippa! He's only going to be in for the night. He's not really ill, you know, and he'll sleep soundly now.'

She bit her lip. She was reacting hysterically. No one would ever guess that she was a qualified nurse and had been halfway to becoming a doctor! She shook her head. 'Of course. Take no notice of me.'

A little later, seeing Simon happily settled in the children's ward, looking peaceful now and breathing normally through his transparent oxygen mask, Philippa gave a sigh of relief. Dropping a kiss on his forehead and promising to come again in the morning, she whispered her thanks to the nurse and tiptoed out. In the corridor Peter was waiting. He took her arm.

'Come on – you need a coffee. We can get one in the cafeteria downstairs. I've telephoned to see if there were any messages and it seems things are quiet for the moment.'

Seated opposite him at one of the little plastic-topped tables, Philippa looked at her ex-fiancé properly for the first time. He was wearing his dark hair shorter and he had put on a little weight, she noticed, but that was to his advantage; he had always been too thin. Being married obviously suited him. She studied the clever face with its high forehead and straight nose, wondering for the first time what he was doing, acting as locum for Doctor Martin. The last she had heard he had been all set to study for a degree in pharmacology. Medical research had been his burning ambition.

He caught her looking at him and smiled ruefully. 'Well – small world, isn't it?'

She nodded. 'You were the last person I was expecting to see.' She stirred her coffee thoughtfully. 'Laura died a few months ago – pneumonia,' she explained briefly. 'That's why we're here. I'm sharing a house with an old school friend.'

'Oh – I'm sorry, love.' Peter put his hand

over hers and gave it a sympathetic squeeze. 'So now you're bringing the boy up alone?'

She nodded. 'I've got a job at a local health centre – nurse/receptionist. It works quite well. Dorcas – my friend – is a teacher at the school Simon goes to, you see; so one of us is always with him.' She looked up to find him looking pensive. 'I expect you're thinking, what a waste,' she pre-empted defensively.

He shook his head. 'No – more like "the best laid plans..."' He smiled wryly at her. 'I've changed course myself. I've grown up a little since last we met, Pippa; had one or two knocks of my own.'

'Your degree?' She looked at him enquiringly.

'To name but one!' he told her. 'Unfortunately I wasn't able to convince the powers that be to let me have a grant and I couldn't afford to do it without.'

'I'm sorry. And – Caroline. Surely you must be married by now?'

He pulled a face. 'There again...' He shrugged. 'No need to go into detail. Enough to say that it would never have worked. You see, in spite of being a doctor's daughter, Caroline wasn't doctor's wife material, though that was only one of the problems.' He looked into her eyes. 'I think the real trouble was that it was very much a rebound thing on my part.' He smiled wistfully at her. 'Things have a way of working out for the best, if only one could see it at the time. Pippa...' he looked intently at her, 'what I'm trying to admit is that I realise now that however dedicated you are it isn't possible to go through life on a single track. A certain amount of compromise is inevitable. Since I last saw you I've learned that the hard way. I've had both the time and the opportunity to realise what you must have gone through.' He glanced at her gravely. 'And how little I contributed in the way of help.'

Very gently Philippa pulled her hand from under his, avoiding his eyes. 'It's all water under the bridge now, Peter,' she said awkwardly. She sipped her coffee and asked, changing the subject: 'How long will you be here?'

'At least another week,' he told her. 'Doctor Martin has had a bad attack of shingles, but he's on the mend now. This is a kind of experiment, by the way,' he explained. 'If I find the work satisfying – and so far I have – I'm going back to take a GP course. I dare say you're thinking it's high time I made up my mind to settle down.' He grinned that half-forgotten boyish grin that lit up the grey eyes, lifting the corners of the rather serious mouth, and suddenly Philippa was transported back to the carefree days of her training. They had had such fun together in those far-off, magic days when life lay before them, smooth and uncomplicated. She felt a twinge of bitter-sweet sadness for a time gone for ever. They were both totally different people now. She had never realised it as intensely as at that moment. For a second they looked at each other and Philippa felt a small uneasiness beginning to steal over her. 'About Simon,' she asked. 'Do you really think it's an allergy? Those kittens mean such a lot to him. I'd hate to have to tell him he had to part with them.'

'Time will tell,' he said. 'The best thing would be to arrange for some skin tests, then you'd know for sure. But if it happens again the moment he gets home it'll be pretty conclusive.'

Philippa looked at her watch and stood up. 'I suppose we'd better be getting back.'

'You're right.' Peter got to his feet and slipped an arm around her. 'You look all in. Better get some rest.'

They were on their way out of the building

when the electronically operated doors opened and a tall man hurried in, head lowered. Philippa's heart skipped a beat as she recognised him. Lifting his head, he saw them and stopped dead. 'Oh – good evening.' His voice was cool and formal, but the slight lift of his eyebrows told her what he was thinking as he took in their apparent intimacy, his eyes pausing on Peter's arm, draped casually over her shoulders.

'Hello, Brent.' Hurriedly, Philippa introduced them: 'This is Doctor Peter Gilbert. He's standing in for Doctor Martin while he's ill. Peter, this is Doctor Brent Charlesworth, one of the partners I work for at Castlebridge Health Centre.'

The two men shook hands, regarding each other guardedly and Peter explained: 'We've just brought Pippa's small nephew in – suffering from an asthmatic attack.'

'Oh – I see.' Brent looked sharply at Philippa. 'Sorry to hear that. I'm here to check a patient in the GP Unit. Do you want me to have a look at him?'

'No need for that. I've given him some Pethidine and the consultant will look at him in the morning,' said Peter. 'He's probably asleep by now anyway.'

Although the two men were impeccably

polite to each other, the hostility between them was like electricity in the air, and Philippa suddenly realised that she hadn't explained that she and Peter were old friends. She said quickly: 'Peter and I trained at the same hospital. Isn't it a coincidence that we should meet like this? I was so surprised to see him...' Too late she realised that she had probably only made the situation worse.

'I see – well, I'd better go up and see my patient,' Brent said briskly. 'Nice to have met you, Doctor Gilbert. Goodnight.'

As they crossed the car park Philippa was silent and as they headed homeward in his car Peter asked perceptively: 'New boyfriend?'

Philippa replied, a little too casually, 'Good heavens, no! Whatever makes you think that?'

He smiled, his eyes still on the road. 'Oh, just something about the way he looked at you. And, what's more to the point, the way he looked at *me!*'

As they drew up outside the house Peter turned to her. 'I'd like very much to see you again before I leave, Pippa,' he said, sliding an arm along the back of the seat. 'It's been wonderful, meeting like this, but it would be nice to meet under happier circumstances.'

She smiled. 'I'd like that too, Peter.'

'Fine. I'll be in touch, then – perhaps we can have dinner one evening. And don't worry about Simon. I'm sure he'll be fine.'

Philippa watched the car drive away with a heavy heart. If this had happened just a few short weeks ago she would probably have been over the moon with happiness – but that was when her heart was still her own to give. Brent's unsmiling face in the hospital foyer still haunted her; the mouth tightly drawn and the expressive eyes ice-cool and green. Once more it seemed he was all too ready to draw his own conclusions.

Dorcas was out of her mind with anxiety, but Philippa soon managed to assure her that there was nothing seriously wrong with Simon. 'We may have to find a new home for the kittens, though,' she told her friend sadly. 'I don't know what effect that will have on him.' Suddenly the pent-up emotion of the whole evening overtook her and she sank into a chair and burst into tears. At once Dorcas was beside her, an arm round her shoulders.

'Oh, don't cry, love. He'll be all right. You know how kids can scare you. As for the kittens, we'll think of something. It may not even be that.'

Philippa gulped back her tears, feeling foolish. Tears were a luxury she hadn't indulged in for a long time. There hadn't been much point in self-pity when there was no one to care. 'Simon's attack wasn't all that happened this evening,' she told Dorcas as she fumbled for a handkerchief. 'Doctor Martin is ill and his locum came instead. He turned out to be – Peter Gilbert, of all people.' Dorcas's mouth dropped open in surprise and Philippa went on, 'He was very kind and I was so glad to have someone I knew to look at Simon. I didn't even think about what seeing him again might mean until after the crisis was over. Then, when we were coming out of the hospital, who should we run into but Brent!'

'Don't tell me – he jumped to the wrong conclusion again!' Dorcas shook her head at Philippa. 'Honestly, Pippa, that man hasn't an ounce of trust in him! If I were you I'd tell him to take a running jump. He doesn't deserve a girl like you.' Her frown dissolved into a smile. 'But what about Peter – is he married now? What's he doing here...?'

Philippa found herself telling her friend all that Peter had told her. By the time she had finished she found that a lot of the tension had ebbed out of her.

'And you're going out to dinner with him too?' beamed Dorcas. 'Well now, that's what I *call* a development! Didn't it cheer you up?'

Philippa shook her head. 'I don't know. I'm not sure how I feel about it at the moment,' she said slowly.

Dorcas looked at her for a long moment. 'I was right, wasn't I? You are in love with Brent.'

'It would never work,' Philippa said despairingly. 'We've been out of step from the start and now we can't seem to get near each other. It's as though there's a barrier between us. It's like a ten-foot wall.'

For a moment Dorcas was silent, then she said with a wry smile, 'Well, love, if you want my advice, for what it's worth, it's this: If you can't knock the damned wall down, then one of you is going to have to climb over!'

The following morning Philippa was just leaving the house when the telephone rang. She hesitated in the doorway. Should she ignore it? A thought struck her: It could be the hospital about Simon. Stepping back inside and closing the door, she lifted the receiver.

It wasn't the hospital. It was Peter. 'Ah, Pippa, I'm glad I caught you. I've just been on to the hospital and spoken to the paediatric registrar. He says they're not all that busy at the moment and they'll run some skin tests on Simon today, before they discharge him. It'll save you having to wait and bring him in for an appointment. I said I'd check with you first, though. Is that all right?'

'Fine. Thank you, Peter,' she said gratefully. 'I do appreciate all you've done.'

'It's a pleasure.' There was a pause, then he said: 'Pippa, about that dinner date; would Monday be all right? I know it's not a very festive sort of day, and I'd have preferred to see you over the weekend, but Monday is my one evening off next week.'

Philippa's heart quickened with apprehension. Did she want to go out to dinner with Peter? Would it force her into making an awkward decision?

'I'll book a table,' he went on. 'Is there any place you particularly like?'

She sighed. He had been so good over Simon. Maybe he felt as she did, that their affair was over and dead. Maybe she was attaching too much importance to his invitation. After all, next week he would be gone. 'Monday would be fine, thank you, Peter,' she said. 'I don't mind where we go. I'll have to fly now, though, or I'll be late.'

'Great. I'll pick you up about eight, then. 'Bye!'

When Philippa arrived at the Centre Brent was in the office collecting his mail. He looked up at her in surprise. 'I didn't expect you to come in this morning,' he told her. 'Don't you want to go to the hospital to be with your – with Simon?'

Jenny turned, looking from one to the other in alarm, obviously wondering what had happened.

Philippa shook her head calmly. 'He won't be coming out until after lunch. Peter – Doctor Gilbert rang me just as I was leaving home. They're going to run some skin tests on Simon this morning. He arranged it for me.'

A flicker of irritation crossed Brent's face, but he made no comment. 'You'd better take the afternoon off, then.' He looked at Jenny. 'I'm sure Jenny wouldn't mind standing in for you for once.'

'Of course I wouldn't,' the girl put in. 'And if there's anything else I can do to help...' She looked at Philippa. 'What's happened?'

Philippa began to take off her coat. 'An

asthma attack,' she explained. 'It's probably some sort of allergy, that's why they're doing the tests. I'm afraid it might be the two kittens we acquired recently and I'm dreading having to tell Simon he'll have to part with them.'

'Oh dear. It never rains but it pours, does it? You seem to be having more than your share of...' Jenny winced as Brent went out, slamming the door behind him. 'Ooh! What's the matter with him this morning?' she asked, eyebrows raised.

Philippa had just finished changing into her uniform when there was a tap on the door and it opened to admit Brent. 'Are you on emergency duty tomorrow morning?' he asked. She shook her head. 'Good, so you'll have the whole weekend to spend with Simon?'

'That's right,' she told him.

He came into the room and closed the door behind him. 'I'd rather like to see him,' he said hesitantly. 'Asthma in children is something that interests me. I've one or two theories that might...'

'But surely that wouldn't be ethical, would it?' queried Philippa. 'After all, he is someone else's patient.'

He coloured. 'When I said "see him!", I

197

meant as a friend – purely as a matter of interest,' he told her. 'Naturally I wouldn't dream of treating him.'

She bit her lip. Why was it that everything she said seemed to rub him up the wrong way – and how was it that he seemed determined to put her in her place? 'I – think it might be better to let him get over it for the present,' she said. 'Anyway, I don't want him used as a guinea-pig.' The moment she had said it she knew she had gone too far.

Brent caught his breath sharply, his brows gathering into a frown. 'Is that really how it sounded? If so I'm sorry. Please forget I suggested it.'

She began to get up as he turned to leave, appalled at her own tactlessness. 'Oh! Please, I didn't mean…' But it was too late. She found herself speaking to the closed door.

It was as Philippa was tidying up after surgery that Nick Cornish put his head round the door. Her heart sank when she saw him; she wasn't in the mood for his heavy-handed brand of humour this morning. He sat down in her chair and put his feet up on her desk. 'Thought you'd like to know that I think I've got a place for old

Mrs Haytor,' he told her.

She stared at him. 'A place – where?'

'Riverside Haven. She's lucky, it's one of the newest of the Council homes.'

Philippa frowned. 'But has something happened that I haven't heard about?'

He sighed. 'Oh, come on, Philippa, the poor old dear can't manage. She can barely see – *or* hear – and when I looked in on her the other day she was so confused she didn't even know who I was. I thought it was time someone did something about her.'

'Have you contacted her daughter?' Philippa asked fearfully.

He shook his head. 'No, not yet. I'm still waiting for confirmation of this place.'

'Look, let me go and see her first,' she urged him. 'I'm sure you're making a mistake. I saw her just a few days ago and she was fine then.'

He pulled a face. 'Oh, Philippa, what's the difference? Now or in six months – it's only a matter of time before she has to give up. Better for her to go in now, while she's okay, than to have an accident and be forced to go.'

'Did you give her the choice?' she demanded. 'Have you even *suggested* it to her?'

'I told you, she was too confused.'

She faced him angrily, the tensions of the morning suddenly snapping her patience. 'Do you have any idea what it's like to have everything taken away from you?' she demanded. 'Your home, your dignity, your independence? Do you have any idea what that means to someone like Mrs Haytor who's never asked anyone for anything in her life – who has the kind of pride and integrity that few people nowadays...'

'*Hang on!*' Nick got to his feet to glare at her. 'I'm only trying to do my *job*, you know. No need to make me sound like some kind of Nazi stormtrooper!'

Philippa bit her lip. She seemed to do nothing lately but put people's backs up. 'Sorry. It's just that you don't seem to have the knack of putting yourself in other people's shoes, Nick. Just let me go and see her, that's all I ask.'

He was only half appeased. 'If you don't mind my saying so, I can't see that it has anything to do with you,' he told her bluntly. 'But – all right.' He turned to her at the door. 'Only don't blame me if something happens to her! I only hope you know what you're making yourself responsible for!'

Philippa sighed as he breezed out of the

room, leaving the door swinging on its hinges in a way that was typical of him. He was right, she told herself. She should have left it to him. She was interfering in something that didn't concern her. Anyone would think she hadn't enough problems of her own to cope with!

'I'm sorry, but I couldn't help overhearing most of that.'

She looked up wearily to see Brent standing in the doorway. 'Oh, I suppose you think I'm interfering too,' she said defensively. 'It seems to be my week for putting my foot in it.'

'As a matter of fact I agree with you,' he told her quietly, coming into the room and closing the door. 'Nick may have the best of intentions, but you know what they say about *them* – the road to hell and so on. Personally, I don't think he has enough experience of life to understand all the situations he has to deal with. I went to see Mrs Haytor myself last week on Greg's day off and I was most impressed with the way she was coping.'

Philippa looked up at him. 'You agree, then – that it would be a tragedy to put her into a home?'

He nodded. 'I do. Some old people take to it well – the company, being looked after, but not Mrs Haytor. In six months she'd have drifted into apathy; six more and senility would have set in. You seem to get along well with her. Go and see her, Philippa. Check that she really is all right and if you think she's managing I'll back you up.'

She hesitated. 'Nick was right in one thing. It isn't really my place...'

'All right, we'll get the opinion of the health visitor too. But I have a strong feeling hers will match yours.'

She looked at him, realising that for once they were actually agreeing about something. Work seemed to be their only common ground. For a moment their eyes met and she found herself under the spell of his magnetic blue gaze.

'Brent, I – I'm sorry – for what I said earlier,' she stammered. 'It was pure tactlessness on my part. I didn't mean to imply – that you...' she trailed off as he crossed the room to her.

'When are you going to stop bearing this grudge, Philippa?' he asked. 'I made a mistake about you – more than one. But they were the same mistakes that everyone else made. And you were really to blame, for being so close about yourself.' He took a step towards her. 'I really want to help, can't you see that? Why do you shut me out?'

She couldn't look at him as she said softly: 'I don't want to shut you out. That's the last thing... It's just...'

'Just *pride*,' he finished for her, shaking his head. 'Stupid, stubborn, *maddening* pride!'

She looked up at him, her cheeks warm with colour. 'I've grown used to coping by myself,' she told him angrily. 'Used to broken promises and people who shy away from unwanted responsibility. I've learned that there's only one person in this life you can really rely on, and that's yourself. *That's* why I'm the way I am!'

For a moment Brent looked down at her. 'Quite a speech,' he said dryly. 'Well, let me tell you something, Pippa James – you haven't learned everything life has to teach – not yet you haven't. There seem to be quite a few things for you to *unlearn*, and the sooner you give way a little and allow someone inside that hard little shell of yours, the better.' He looked down at her, the corners of his mouth relaxing into a smile. 'I'll ask you just once more – may I come and meet Simon tomorrow, if I admit that I'd quite like to see *you* too?' He spread his hands. 'Away from this place, I mean, so that we can relax together and talk.'

His eyes searched hers and she recognised the sincerity in their depths. She nodded, smiling. 'I'm sure both Simon and I would like that very much,' she said. 'Perhaps you'd like to come to lunch?'

'I would – very much.'

'Around twelve?'

'Around twelve it shall be.' For a moment they looked into each other's eyes, then he pulled her close and kissed her. It was a brief, hard kiss that left her a little breathless, but it was enough to lend wings to her flagging spirits and send her on her way with a lighter heart.

CHAPTER TEN

It wasn't until they sat relaxing that evening after Simon was in bed that Philippa felt free to tell Dorcas what had taken place at the hospital that afternoon.

'I saw the paediatric registrar when I collected Simon after lunch,' she said, 'and he told me that the result of the skin tests had been negative. Simon hadn't reacted to any of the most common irritants. And that included cats.'

Dorcas looked thoughtful. 'And yet, the moment he got home and started to play with the kittens again he started to wheeze. Did you notice?'

'Of course I did.' Philippa sighed. 'I didn't mention it to him, though. If he starts being anxious himself it will only aggravate matters. I can't help worrying, though.' She looked up at her friend. 'Oh, by the way, I've invited Brent to lunch tomorrow. It seems he has some theories about asthma in children.'

Dorcas looked sceptical. 'Oh, really? I hope

they're better than some of his other theories!'

'We had a talk this morning,' Philippa told her. 'I really think he wants to make up for the – misunderstanding.'

Dorcas raised an eyebrow. 'What about Peter? I thought you were going out to dinner with him.'

'Oh, I am,' Philippa told her. 'We arranged it on the telephone this morning. But he's on call all weekend. It's to be on Monday.' She saw Dorcas looking at her and added, 'It's only for old times' sake, Dorcas.'

'Ah, but does *he* know that? And have you told Brent?'

Philippa got up and began to move restlessly round the room. 'The two things are completely unrelated,' she argued. 'Brent is coming to meet Simon and – and to…'

'*Codswallop!*' exploded Dorcas. 'My God, Pippa, you seem to have a positive *genius* for complicating life! It might all be clear and above board as far as you're concerned, but people aren't mind-readers, you know! Especially men,' she added darkly. 'In my experience they seem to have trouble understanding their own minds, let alone ours!'

'Well, I'll have ample opportunity to mention it to Brent tomorrow,' said Philippa, anxious to dismiss the subject. 'Now, what do you suggest we give him for lunch?'

'Include me out, as they say.' Dorcas got to her feet and moved towards the kitchen. 'I meant to tell you before – John has invited me to go and meet his parents tomorrow. We'll be making an early start as it's quite a long drive, so I think I'll have an early night.'

Philippa stared at her. 'Well! You've kept that quiet. You're going to meet his parents? That sounds quite serious. After what you said, I thought…'

Dorcas paused as she went through the door, looking back over her shoulder, a mischievous glint in her eyes. 'We can all make mistakes, darling – even me! John sort of *grows* on you after a while.' And with this profound remark she made her exit.

Philippa didn't sleep very well that night, lying with one ear alert for the sound of Simon wheezing again. It would be a long time before she forgot the sheer terror of the inadequacy she had felt last night. It had taught her several things. The first was that she loved Simon quite as much as she would ever love a child of her own. Their lives were now inextricably entwined. Nothing and no one would ever part them. The other was that she was a lot more vulnerable than she

207

had admitted – and not just where Simon was concerned. 'They say that love makes you strong enough to face anything,' she whispered into the darkness. 'But it finds all your weaknesses too.'

Dorcas woke her early with a cup of tea. 'It's a pig of a day!' she complained, flopping down on Philippa's bed. 'Just my luck! Freezing cold and raining too. Looks as though it could even turn to snow!' She turned to Philippa who was still rubbing the sleep from her eyes. 'By the way – fish!'

'What?' Philippa sat up, trying to collect her thoughts.

'*Fish!* You asked me last night what you should give His Lordship for lunch. You needn't go out to the shops, there's plenty in the freezer. You could make one of those pies you're so good at with mushrooms and tomatoes and all that crispy potato on top.' She looked wistful. 'Mmm, I'm beginning to wish I was having a cosy day in myself.' She turned to grin at Philippa. 'Don't worry, I'm not planning to play gooseberry. I don't think I could stand the sight of John's disappointed face if I said I wasn't going.' She stood up with a sigh. 'Ah well, I suppose I'd better go and try to make myself glamorous.' She left the room, only to pop her head back round the door a moment later. 'Oh, by the way – the fish. Don't worry, I got some haddock out for you. It's already started to thaw.'

Philippa sank back against the pillow, relaxing with her cup of tea. The problem of lunch, it seemed, was taken care of. Dorcas seemed in a good mood in spite of the weather. It seemed fairly clear that she was beginning to see distinct possibilities in John after all.

An hour later she and Simon waved them off; John looking quite handsome in his smart new suit and Dorcas trying to appear casual about the whole thing, though Philippa guessed that underneath, she was nervous about the coming meeting with his parents. When they had gone she set about making the pie and other preparations for lunch, while Simon 'helped', perching on a kitchen stool to hand her things.

'What's Doctor Charlesworth like, Pippa?' he asked. 'And why is he coming to have lunch with us?'

'Well, he's one of the doctors I work with and he's very nice. I'm sure you'll like him,' she told him. 'He wants very much to meet you.'

Simon looked thoughtful, then asked: 'Are

you going to marry him?'

She looked at him. '*Simon!* Whatever gave you that idea?'

He regarded her, head on one side, his little face deadly serious. 'Darren – he's my second best friend at school – says that his mummy is getting him a new daddy. *He* keeps coming to lunch. Darren's old daddy married another lady a long time ago. But you haven't been married before, have you, Pippa?'

'No.' She lowered her head over the pastry she was making.

'Why haven't you?'

'Well, for one thing, no one asked me,' she told him. 'And for another, I've been too busy.'

He digested this information for a few moments, then asked: 'Pippa, if you did get married would I still belong to you?'

She took a deep breath, frantically searching her mind for an answer that would reassure him. 'You'll always…' The doorbell rang and Simon jumped down from his stool.

'I expect that's him. Can I answer it, please?'

With a sudden rush of nervousness Philippa hastily tidied her hair in front of

210

the kitchen mirror, brushing a streak of flour from her nose and removing her apron. Her heart gave a lurch as she heard Brent's voice in the hall. She took a last look in the mirror, then opened the kitchen door and went to meet him.

He was taking off his coat. On the hall table lay a large square box and a bunch of red roses wrapped in cellophane. He saw her and smiled. 'Hello.'

'Let me have your coat,' she held out her hand. 'It's wet.'

'Only a few drops.' He handed her the roses. 'These are for you.' He looked at Simon. 'And the other is yours. I hope you like jigsaw puzzles.'

Simon's face lit up and he took the parcel and began to tear off the wrapping. 'Oh yes, thank you, I do. Oh, look, Pippa! It's a picture of two kittens just like Tippy and Smudge.' He bore his present off gleefully into the living room and Philippa called:

'Simon! Come and be properly intro-duced. You're forgetting your manners.' Slightly shamefaced, he came back. 'That's better. Now – this is Doctor Charlesworth.'

Solemnly, Simon shook hands and Brent said, 'Doctor Charlesworth is a bit of a mouthful, isn't it? I think you'd better call me Uncle Brent, don't you? I've been look-ing forward to seeing these kittens of yours. Do I get to see them now?'

Philippa watched as Simon happily took Brent's hand and led him into the kitchen where the kittens were curled up together in their box, lulled to sleep by the warmth of Philippa's cooking. She watched the two heads bent over the box and just for a moment her heart was pierced by a deep yearning for something she daren't hope for. Quickly she turned to her saucepans.

'Lunch will be ready in five minutes,' she announced brightly. 'Simon, would you like to ask Doct – Uncle Brent if he would like a sherry and show him where it is?'

Lunch was a great success. Brent insisted that his favourite food was fish and he and Simon got along right from the first. When the last of the apple pie had been cleared from the dish, Philippa rose, announcing that she would make coffee after she had washed up.

'Can we help?' asked Brent.

She shook her head. 'I can manage. And I know that you're both dying to have a go at that puzzle. I'll leave you to it.'

Later, as they sat lazily drinking coffee, watching Simon concentrating on the puzzle,

Samantha arrived and after looking at Philippa for approval, Simon went off to play at his friend's house, well wrapped up in his anorak and wellingtons. When the children had gone Philippa looked at Brent.

'Thank you for being so nice to him.'

He looked surprised. 'He's a nice child. It wasn't an effort on my part. Philippa, I managed to have a talk with him over the jigsaw puzzle. I learned quite a lot.'

'You did?'

'By asking some shamefully leading questions I got some rather interesting answers. I think I can safely say that Simon isn't allergic to cats or any other animals – except perhaps the human kind.'

Eyes wide, she looked at him. 'The tests proved it wasn't the kittens, yet he still wheezes when he comes into close contact with them.'

He moved across to the settee and sat beside her. 'It's a bit more complicated than a straightforward allergy. Since he's been at school it appears he's been talking to the other children. It's inevitable; youngsters are a lot more street-wise nowadays than we were at their age. Divorce and one-parent families are all too common nowadays. Apparently he's gathered that when you have no mother or father at all, you have to be adopted – just like he "adopted" the motherless kittens. And I believe that it was this that triggered the asthma off.'

Philippa looked at him, appalled. 'You mean he thinks I might hand him over to another family? But why didn't he talk to me about this?'

Brent shook his head. 'I'm sure you know that the closest person to you isn't always the easiest person to talk to. And when something scares you that much there's always the feeling that talking about it might make it happen,' he told her. 'He found it much easier to tell me – a stranger.' He paused. 'There's something else. He's a perceptive child and he realises that you might want to marry.'

She recalled the conversation they'd had before Brent arrived and nodded. 'He *has* mentioned that to me – just before lunch this morning, as it happens.'

He looked at her enquiringly. 'And what did you tell him?'

She coloured. 'I – didn't have time to think of an answer. Just at that moment you arrived.'

Brent grinned. 'Saved by the bell, eh? What would your answer have been – if you'd had time to give it?'

Philippa moistened her dry lips, then said firmly, 'That it wouldn't make any difference to us. I'd never let Simon down no matter what. I lost...' She moistened her lips and began again. 'I've made one sacrifice for him, after all.'

He looked into her eyes for a long moment, his expression impossible for her to read. Finally he said: 'I think you must be prepared for him to have these asthma attacks until he feels more secure, Philippa. He's a sensitive child. He probably senses something in the air. I'd try to put him straight if I were you.'

She looked away. Put Simon straight! If only she could. At the moment she felt she needed someone to straighten out her own turbulent thoughts and emotions!

Samantha and Simon arrived back in a flurry of wet anoraks and muddy wellingtons and it was time for tea. Simon begged Brent to stay and they had hot buttered toast, tea and jam sponge in front of the fire, after which Samantha was packed off home and Simon was sent up to get ready for bed.

Standing in the doorway, he looked back. 'Uncle Brent, will you come up and read me a story?'

Philippa blushed with embarrassment. 'Simon! You hardly know Doctor Charlesworth. You shouldn't ask...'

Brent interrupted her with a smile. 'Of course I'll come up and read you a story, Simon. We're old friends, aren't we?'

Simon looked at Philippa triumphantly. 'See?' His eyes widened. 'Is that all right?'

She relented, laughingly. 'All right then, off you go – and mind you remember to clean your teeth.'

While Brent was upstairs with Simon she washed up the tea things and straightened the living room, putting away the half completed jigsaw. As she went about these small domestic tasks she couldn't help fantasising a little, thinking how cosy it would be if this was her own home – hers and Simon's and – and... She pulled herself up abruptly, chiding herself for foolish daydreams. Anyone would think she was a teenager with her head in the clouds, rather than a woman with more than her share of worldly problems!

Brent reappeared as she was looking in the sideboard cupboard to see what she could offer him in the way of a drink. 'We read his favourite book, the one about the space monster,' he told her with a smile. 'Do you

216

know, I really enjoyed it. Stories aren't all that different from the ones I used to enjoy. It's like mythology with hi-tech instead of magic.' He sat down on the settee and held out his hand to her. 'Come and sit down.'

'I've been looking to see what I could offer you to drink,' she told him. 'I'm afraid there isn't much of a choice. I've only got some rather mediocre sherry or whisky and ginger.'

He shook his head. 'Don't worry about it now. I'd like to talk.' He took her hand and pulled her down beside him on the settee. 'I was wondering whether there was anything you wanted to ask me?'

She shook her head, realising that he was referring to her remark about his relationship with Emma the other day. She bit her lip. 'It's none of my business. I shouldn't have…'

'All right then,' he cut in impatiently. 'If you won't ask, I'll tell you about it anyway. There've been enough misunderstandings between us.' He took her hand and held it very firmly, as though he was afraid she might move away. 'Emma and I have known each other since childhood, and two years ago, when I first came back to join the group practice at the Health Centre, there seemed to be a general feeling that we might make a good couple.'

Philippa shifted uneasily. 'Please, Brent. There's no need...'

He continued, ignoring her protests. 'I made it quite clear to her from the first that marriage wasn't among my plans and that we were never likely to be anything more than friends – at least, I *thought* I'd made it clear. We saw quite a lot of each other. For me it was very pleasant to have a woman companion I knew so well. I could relax with Emma. In my naïve way I thought it uncomplicated.' He sighed. 'I suppose I should have seen what was coming – should have realised how her feelings were developing, and when at last she told me I was appalled at my own lack of perception. God only knows I'd no wish to hurt her.' He shrugged. 'To cut a long story short, her cruise was supposed to help her forget me, and I think it worked. Having dinner with her the other evening showed me that she's developed a lot as a person. This new job she's got is widening her horizons considerably.' He drew in his breath and his brow creased. 'There is one thing that worries me slightly, though...' He smiled and shook his head. 'But I'm sure you're not interested in my worries.'

'No, tell me about it. Maybe I can help,' Philippa insisted.

Brent smiled, slipping an arm around her shoulders. 'I doubt it, it's probably just my suspicious nature, but I'll tell you anyway. A while ago my mother wanted to give me a seat on the board of directors at Express-lines. I turned it down. Now I'm wondering if this is her way of trying to win me round. She's hoping that Emma will have better powers of persuasion.' He gave a dry little laugh. 'I wouldn't be surprised if Aunt Angela didn't have a hand in it too!'

Philippa was intrigued, her mind going back to the remarks Angela Stone had made that evening at Brent's flat. Privately, she wondered if the two women weren't doing a spot of matchmaking – plotting to get Brent and Emma back together again. 'Why wouldn't you join the firm?' she asked. She saw his mouth harden as he replied:

'I don't feel I owe that firm anything – my mother either, seeing that she *is* the firm.' He turned to look at her and she saw the bitterness in his eyes. 'My childhood was sacrificed to CEL,' he told her. 'I'd scarcely had time to get over the death of my father when I found that I'd lost my family life and my mother too. She allowed her interest in the business to swallow it all up. It became a positive obsession. If it hadn't been for Aunt Angela, God knows what would have happened to me. Even when I qualified she didn't try to disguise the fact that it was a disappointment to her that I hadn't gone into the business!' His arm about her shoulders tightened. 'Now perhaps you can understand why I feel such a rapport with Simon.' He turned to look at her. 'And why I admire all that you've done, Philippa.'

She looked away. *'Admire'*. It was the second time he'd used that word. She had had her share of admiration and found it remote and sterile. It set her apart like a stone statue on a pedestal. Admiration was for paragons, and she was no paragon – far from it! 'I think you've got quite the wrong idea about me, Brent,' she told him slowly. 'I did – what I did because there was no one else to do it at the time, not out of sheer unselfishness as most people like to imagine. You might as well know that there were times when I felt really sorry for myself; times when I wept with anger and frustration at the sheer unfairness of it all.' Her voice rose and gathered momentum as the words tumbled out. 'At times like that I didn't give a thought to poor Laura and what she had lost – or Simon either for that matter – all I cared about were my own lost opportunities, my ruined life!' She turned to look at him defiantly, trying to swallow the tears that welled up in her throat. *There! Now you know what I'm really like. Can you admire a person like that?'* The last words came out on the crest of a choking sob and he pulled her into his arms and held her close, cradling her head with one large, firm hand, pressing her face into his shoulder as she struggled for control.

'Thank God! I was beginning to think you were made of stone!'

She looked up at him in surprise and he shook his head impatiently. 'For God's sake, Philippa, you wouldn't be human if you hadn't felt those things. You've no business feeling guilty about them!' He shook her gently. 'For heaven's sake let go and cry!' he commanded. 'Stop bottling it all up. You've obviously been doing that far too long. Let it all come out, and never mind about me.'

It was a tremendous relief just simply to do as he said. She snuffled into his shoulder like a little girl; crying for herself, for Paul and Laura and Simon; for all the world's injustices and disappointments; the pent-up emotion of the past two years spilling out of her, leaving her at last feeling drained, yet cleansed and light and free. As the sobs subsided Brent gently lifted her tear-stained face, a finger under her chin.

'Better now?' His eyes smiled down into hers and he handed her a clean folded handkerchief from his pocket. 'Here, better use this.'

She sniffed, accepting and using the handkerchief. 'Thanks. I'm all right now.' She dabbed at her face. 'I don't know what you must think of me.' For the first time she thought about her red eyes and shiny nose and made a movement as though to rise.

He held her firmly. 'Stay where you are. I think you need that whisky now. I'll get it for you.' He bent and kissed her, very gently at first, then as he felt her arms go around his neck he drew her closer, kissing her deeply. 'Admiration was the trigger word, wasn't it?' he whispered, his lips warm against her cheek. 'I'm making no apologies for using it. I *do* admire you, Philippa, but it's more than the cool and distant emotion you imagine. The way I feel has nothing at all to do with being noble and unselfish.' He kissed her again. 'All I want right at this moment is to be with you, to hold you like this. Right at this moment, all I want is to go on kissing you.'

Time seemed to stand still in the moments that followed. For Philippa everything else faded into insignificance except his lips on hers and the exciting rhythm of their hearts, beating in unison. She was still lost in the wonder and ecstasy of it when the front door slammed and excited voices were heard in the hall. Reluctantly they moved apart as the living room door flew open and the overhead light was snapped on abruptly.

Dorcas stood in the doorway, her cheeks pink and her eyes sparkling. Behind her John hung back shyly. Oblivious of having interrupted anything of importance, she announced: 'Guess what – no, don't bother, I can't wait to tell you. We're engaged! John and I are going to be married!'

CHAPTER ELEVEN

'You seemed surprised at the news of your friend's engagement, Pippa?' Brent's eyes were on the road ahead.

'A little, perhaps,' Philippa looked thoughtful as she sat beside him in the passenger seat of the Porsche. After drinking a toast to the newly engaged couple's health, they had tactfully withdrawn. Brent suggesting that as they hadn't been out all day they should slip out for a drink. 'I knew John was keen,' she went on, 'but Dorcas seemed wary after the failure of her first marriage.'

'Sometimes I wonder if too much pressure is put on people to be married,' said Brent. 'We see so many marriages break up. I'd go so far as to say that among the twenty to thirty age group eighty per cent of our patients' problems are to do with divorce or marital problems.'

Philippa shot him a sidelong glance. 'You're against it, then?'

'Against the problems it causes,' he corrected. 'I think people take it far too lightly

– go into it under the assumption that they can always divorce if it doesn't work out. They don't realise how traumatic and destructive that can be. Or the terrible effect it can have on their children.' Philippa said nothing and he turned to her. 'By the way, I've been wanting to ask you – Doctor Peter Gilbert – is he…?'

'Yes,' she said quickly. 'Peter is the man I gave up along with my career after my brother's accident.'

He was silent for a moment, negotiating a traffic island as he headed for the ring road. 'Quite a coincidence,' he remarked dryly, 'his turning up here as Doctor Martin's locum, I mean. It must have been a shock for you both – meeting again like that.'

'Yes, it was.' Philippa bit her lip. She found herself suddenly tongue-tied; unable to think of an appropriate remark. Her first instinct had been to tell him exactly how she had felt – cool and unemotional, simply glad to see Peter as a doctor and an old friend. She wanted to tell him how seeing Peter again had confirmed for her that everything that had existed between them was well and truly dead. But the words he had spoken a few moments ago made her hesitate. Could it be that he shared Peter's views about responsibility? He had said that marriage wasn't among his plans. It seemed that he too was unprepared for the inevitable problems of sharing one's life – unwilling to take the risks involved. Perhaps the last thing he wanted was to hear her declare that what she had felt for Peter was quite dead. It might make him fear that, like Emma's, her own feelings for him were becoming too intense. She cleared her throat and said lightly: 'A very pleasant shock, though.'

Brent glanced at her briefly. 'I see. I wondered... Damn!' He braked sharply, noticing in the nick of time that the traffic lights had turned red.

They had a drink in a rather flashy pub on the outskirts of the town, but the mood of the evening had changed; suddenly neither of them knew what to say to one another. Philippa was acutely aware that things had gone wrong between them, yet not quite sure why. It seemed that everything she said made it worse rather than better, and she was almost relieved when Brent looked at his watch and asked her if she was ready to leave. Back in the car her heart felt like lead. The day had begun so well, everything had been fine till Dorcas and John had arrived and broken their news. Now it was ruined.

Bleakly, she wondered if Brent knew the reason; she certainly didn't.

Sunday was a strange day. John arrived early and bore Dorcas off to have lunch with friends, and Simon was invited to Samantha's for the day. Philippa found herself wandering listlessly round the house, staring unseeingly out of windows, unable to concentrate on anything. Perhaps Brent saw her as a colleague – a female companion with whom he had medicine in common – nothing more than that. She tried hard to adjust to the fact. Angrily, she threw herself into a frenzy of housework – anything to occupy her mind and use up her energy. But she had done all there was to do by mid-morning. The rest of the day stretched ahead endlessly. Suddenly she thought of someone else for whom Sunday might seem a long day. Making up her mind, she put on her coat and set off for Heather Road.

As Philippa tapped on the back door of number eleven Heather Road she could smell beef roasting. There couldn't be a lot wrong with Mrs Haytor, she told herself, if she still bothered to cook herself a Sunday dinner! After a moment or two the door opened a crack and the old lady peered out.

'Who is it? Oh, it's you, my dear!' She beamed delightedly at Philippa and opened the door wider. 'Do come in. You're just in time for a cup of coffee.'

Philippa stepped inside the neat kitchen and looked around her. Everything looked spick-and-span. For the first time she wondered what excuse she could make for calling on the old lady on a Sunday morning. She needn't have worried. Mrs Haytor saved her the trouble.

'I dare say that young whippersnapper has been telling tales about me,' she remarked as she poured coffee into two cups. She looked up at Philippa and gave a wicked chuckle. 'I overdid it that time, I reckon!' She pulled out a chair. 'Sit down, love. I think I'd better tell you all about it.'

Philippa did as she was told, relieved to see that the old lady was far from confused this morning. 'Mr Cornish was a little worried about you,' she confessed. 'So I promised I'd look in on you to make sure that you didn't need help of any kind.'

The old lady gave a little bark of laughter. 'Get away with you! He told you I was ga-ga and ought to be put away! Go on now – admit it.'

Taken aback, Philippa shook her head. 'That's putting it a little strongly, Mrs Haytor.'

'I'll tell you a little secret,' said Mrs Haytor, tapping one side of her nose conspiratorially. 'When I was staying with Maureen, my daughter, after I came out of hospital, I found that if I turned off my hearing aid and sat with my eyes closed they stopped bothering me – thought I was asleep, see? It worked a treat!'

Philippa began to see the light. 'Ah! And that's what you did with Nick – Mr Cornish. Well, I'm afraid it backfired this time, Mrs Haytor.'

The faded blue eyes twinkled. 'I shall have to be on my best behaviour next time he calls, won't I?' she teased. 'Never mind, love. I always did enjoy living dangerously!' She cackled merrily at the joke. 'Come on, have another cup of coffee before you go.'

Philippa's heart was lighter as she made her way home. It would have been very sad to have seen such a plucky old lady forced to give up her independence.

On Monday morning she was just changing into her uniform when there was a tap on her door and Sister Taggart bustled unceremoniously in. She took in Philippa's state of half undress and apologised briefly.

'Oh, sorry to barge in like that, Nurse, but I'm up to my neck. Just wanted to have a word with you about the Brown girl – Sandra.' Noticing Philippa's blank expression, she added: 'Oh, obviously you haven't heard. She had the baby yesterday – almost a month prematurely; a five-pound girl. I delivered her, with Doctor Charlesworth standing by. She had a very rough time, poor lass.' She sniffed. 'I think that's one little mistake she won't repeat in a hurry!'

'Is she all right?' asked Philippa. 'And the baby?'

Sister Taggart's face softened. 'The baby's the prettiest little thing you ever saw,' she said. 'But Sandra doesn't seem very interested now that it's born. That's why I wondered if you'd go and see her.'

'Me?' Philippa looked at the midwife in surprise.

'Yes. She seems on the verge of agreeing to the child being adopted, but you know me.' She gave Philippa a wry smile. 'Never did have much time for ditherers. I'll just lose patience and muck the whole thing up if I try and persuade her. I think you might pull it off, though. She seems to have a lot of

231

time for you. Will you go and see her – ask her if she'll agree to letting the baby go to a foster-home?'

'Well, I'll do what I can...' Philippa agreed. 'But I thought we were short of foster-parents.'

'Ah, that's just it,' Sister Taggart said eagerly. 'Mrs Hunter – you know, Helen – has put her name down for fostering. They'd like to adopt, but we've advised them to try fostering for a while first. If she took this baby there might be a good chance of adopting it later, if everything works out all right.'

'But supposing Sandra decides she wants the baby back?' asked Philippa. 'Helen has had so many heartbreaks already.'

'I feel fairly certain that once she gets back into her old carefree way of life, Sandra will be only too happy to agree to adoption,' the midwife said shrewdly. 'And I know it'd be a load off her mother's mind. But just for now, would you talk to her – preferably while she's still in hospital and on her own. She and her mother seem determined to be at odds with one another.'

Philippa went to the hospital between lunch and visiting time, getting Jenny to stay on at the Centre an extra half hour until her return. She found Sandra sitting up in bed looking bored and depressed. The girl brightened when she saw that she had a visitor.

'Hello. Fancy seeing you.'

'How are you, Sandra?' Philippa sat down beside the bed. 'I heard all about you this morning from Sister Taggart.'

Sandra pulled a face. 'It was awful! I've got five stitches and they hurt like mad. No one ever told me it'd be that bad, not even Mum. I'm never going to have another!'

Philippa smiled. 'Everyone says that.'

The girl grimaced. 'Not in here they don't. It's all they can talk about. Babies, babies, babies, from morning till night. You'd think no one'd ever had one before. They make me sick!'

'Never mind, you'll be going home in a day or two.'

Sandra slumped, looking even more depressed at the prospect. 'Mum keeps on and on, Nurse James. I'd really made up my mind to get a place of my own. I thought it'd be all right till I saw all those other unmarried mums at the day nursery. Now I just don't know.' A tear squeezed out from the corner of her eye to trickle down her cheek, and Philippa felt her heart give a

233

little twist. The girl looked so young and childlike sitting there in her cotton nightie with her long fair hair hanging limply round her shoulders. She reached out to touch her hand.

'What happened, Sandra?' she asked gently. 'What about the baby's father? What went wrong?'

Sandra gulped. 'He was nice to me – you know – *kind.*' She looked at Philippa with round brimming eyes, the hard, street-wise expression gone. 'Since Mum and Dad split up nothing's been the same at home. Mum didn't seem to have time for me any more – didn't even seem to want me around half the time. I thought I didn't need anyone, but when I met – when I started going out with *him* I realised what I'd been missing. It was so nice, just being – being *loved.*'

'Was he married?' Philippa asked quietly.

The girl shrugged noncommittally. 'When I knew I was having a baby I felt better in a way. It didn't matter quite so much, him going off me like that, because I'd still have someone to love – someone who *couldn't* leave me...' She shook her head sadly. 'But it isn't as easy as that. I saw that at the nursery.' She picked at the coverlet, trying to find the words to express what she felt. 'It was a shock when I saw her – the baby. I don't know what I expected, but she looks so *little*, so helpless. She scared me.' She turned to Philippa, her eyes full of appeal. 'I've been kidding myself, Nurse James, haven't I? It won't work.'

Philippa watched helplessly as the young girl in the bed struggled with an emotional decision she should never have had to face. She felt angry at the pressures of modern society that had put her in this situation. 'I know someone who would give her a marvellous home, Sandra,' she offered. 'It would only be a foster-home at first, so you'd have plenty of time to think carefully about your future – yours and the baby's.'

Sandra brushed away a tear with her knuckles and snuffled noisily. 'Well off, are they?'

'Not specially, but they'd give the baby everything she needed – including lots of love. They've tried to have babies of their own and can't, you see.'

Sandra took a deep breath and looked at her. 'Okay, then.' She shrugged and added bitterly. 'Wait till I tell Mum! It'll be the first time I've done anything right for her in ages!'

'Your mum does care about you, Sandra,'

Philippa assured her. 'I dare say her own problems have taken a lot of coping with. Maybe she thought you were too grown up to need her any more. Maybe this will bring you closer.'

'Yeah – maybe,' said Sandra without conviction. She had retreated inside her hard little shell again, her child's eyes glazed and hard once more as Philippa wished her goodbye. As she walked out of the ward she wondered if she had helped – or if she had merely created new problems for the girl. In the corridor a staff nurse stopped her.

'You were visiting Sandra Brown, weren't you?' she asked. 'Would you like to see the baby?'

Philippa followed her along the corridor to stare through the glass wall of the nursery at the minute bundle in the cot. Sister Taggart had been right. Sandra's little girl was small and dainty, her skin smooth and pink as a rose petal, her tiny waving hands perfect. She even had a halo of soft blonde hair. Reading her thoughts, the staff nurse said: 'Prems are often like that. Gorgeous, isn't she? None of that red and crumpled new-born look.'

Philippa smiled. 'Perhaps she'll be luckier than her mother,' she said. 'I hope so.'

236

As she sat in the office that afternoon she had a lot to think about: Simon, Mrs Haytor; Sandra and her baby. Brent found her deep in thought when he looked in around three.

'Have I missed the afternoon cuppa?' he asked hopefully. 'I didn't have time for lunch.'

She looked up, her heart giving the familiar leap at the sight of his face.

'I was busy at the hospital most of the day yesterday,' he went on. 'Did Tag tell you that Sandra Brown had her baby?'

She nodded. 'I popped in to see her just after lunch. She's agreed to let the baby go to a foster-home – for the time being, at least.'

He smiled. 'That's good news. Her mother will be relieved.'

'There's a lot more to Sandra's case than we thought,' Philippa told him unhappily. 'All that teenage sullenness is just a front. She's the unhappy product of a broken home – looking for the love she missed out on after her parents' divorce. All I hope is that she'll learn from her mistake.'

'Mmm, we all have to do that. And it's never easy.' Brent cleared his throat. 'But I didn't come in here to philosophise. I wondered if you'd like to have dinner with me tonight?'

'Oh, I can't, sorry.'

He looked rather taken aback. 'Are you sure? Tonight's my one night free this week.'

It was Peter's one free night too. He had told her so. It would be the last time she would ever see him, and he had been so helpful over Simon. She really couldn't let him down. She shook her head, muttering something about a promise she couldn't break. Deep inside she wondered at her reluctance to tell Brent her date was with Peter. After all, there was absolutely no reason why she shouldn't go out with him. But something – some inexplicable instinct held her back.

He looked at her for a long moment and she felt her cheeks colouring. 'May one ask who your date is with?' he asked at last.

Trapped, Philippa searched her mind for an answer that wasn't quite a lie. 'An old friend is in town for a few hours,' she said tremulously. His eyes searched hers and for a moment she thought he was going to question her further, then a tap on the door heralded Jenny with a tray of steaming teacups and to Philippa's relief the moment passed.

She quite expected Dorcas to have more to say on the subject of her dinner date with Peter, but she didn't; she had been far too preoccupied with her own thoughts since the weekend. Gratefully, Philippa went off to get ready after Simon was in bed. She decided to wear one of her new dresses, a soft angora in a shade of deep garnet red that lent colour to her ivory complexion and made her eyes sparkle. She saw Peter's car draw up as she was applying a touch of perfume and, picking up her coat she ran quietly down the stairs, calling goodbye to Dorcas as she opened the front door and slipped out. As she got into the car she saw the curtain move at Simon's window and glimpsed his little face looking out. She gave him a wave, hoping he wouldn't pester Dorcas for an extra story once she was out of the way.

Peter had booked a table at a smart country hotel, and the food and wine were excellent. Over dinner he talked of his plans, but Philippa hardly took in what he was saying. Watching him, she was wondering how she could have been so hurt at his rejection. He wasn't even as good-looking as she remembered, and in spite of his protestations that he was 'older and wiser' it was clear that his career ambitions were still very much to the fore of his mind. His wife – if he ever married one – would always have to take second place in Peter's life.

After they had eaten they retired to the lounge for coffee. They talked lightly about general practice and Peter's plans, and Philippa was quite relieved when she looked at her watch and found it was almost eleven o'clock. On the drive home Peter made a tentative suggestion that perhaps they might meet again. She shook her head.

'No, Peter, I think we both know, don't we, that we grew out of each other a long time ago?'

He shrugged resignedly. 'If you say so.' He glanced at her. 'You're quite sure we couldn't rekindle what we had?' He turned to smile at her wistfully. 'We had some good times, Pippa.'

She smiled back. 'I know – and I shall always remember them. But they're part of the person I used to be. All that's happened has changed me. I think the same applies to you. We're two totally different people now.'

'Maybe you're right.' As he drew up outside the house he turned to look at her thoughtfully. 'Any chance of you taking up medicine again?' he asked. 'You were one of the brighter students, as I remember. It seems a shame. Now that Simon is older, couldn't you…?' He stopped as he saw her shaking her head.

'I've learned that there are sometimes more important things than ambition, Peter,' she told him. 'Having someone who needs you has its rewards. It isn't always a burden, you know.'

He said nothing, but she saw from the look in his eyes that the barbed remark had found its target. He got out of the car and came round to her side, opening the door and helping her out. As he did so his hands rested on her shoulders and he smiled down into her eyes. 'Even if we are two totally different people, it's been marvellous seeing you again, Pippa,' he said. 'I hope we'll meet again some day. Good luck with whatever you decide to do, darling.'

'Good luck, Peter – and thank you for what you did for Simon.'

It was a light, casual kiss; the kiss of two people who have known each other for a long time. Philippa hardly noticed the car parked on the other side of the road, or the man standing in the shadow of the doorway.

She waved as Peter got back into the car, only turning as it drew away from the kerb.

When she did so, the smile vanished from her face.

Brent was walking down the path to the gate. In the light from the street lamp she saw that his eyes were hard and angry.

CHAPTER TWELVE

'I was on my way home from a call and I wondered if you were home,' said Brent, watching thoughtfully as Peter's car turned the corner and vanished from sight. 'I'm sorry if I interrupted something.' His eyes found hers and Philippa saw that in spite of the cool tone of his voice they were flashing with resentment.

'Of course you didn't interrupt anything,' she told him edgily, searching her bag for her door key. 'Peter will be gone tomorrow. It was just a farewell dinner, that's all.' She reached out to open the gate, but he laid a hand on her arm.

'In that case why couldn't you have said you were meeting him? Why did you feel it was necessary to lie to me about it?'

She swung round to face him. 'I didn't lie!'

His eyebrows rose. 'An old friend is in town for a few hours...?' he quoted, a mocking edge to his voice. 'Why couldn't you just come right out with it and say it was your ex-fiancé?'

Trapped, she blustered: 'I – I don't tell lies.'

'Exactly. That's why I don't understand it.'

Angrily she shook his hand from her arm. 'I'm not answerable to you for everything I do! What right have you to question me like this? If you don't mind, Brent, I'd like to go in now. It's been a long day and I'm tired.'

His hand dropped to his side and he took a step backwards, his eyes darkening. 'I thought I was really getting to know you, Philippa. The other night, I thought you...' He drew in his breath sharply. 'I should have known better, shouldn't I? God knows I should have realised that you couldn't be *that* different from other women!' Turning abruptly, he strode across the road to his car and got in, slamming the door hard. A moment later Philippa was watching it speeding away.

She swallowed the sick feeling of regret. He had every right to be angry about the white lie she had told him. Why *didn't* she tell him this afternoon that she was going out with Peter? She still didn't really understand her own motives. But surely he was overreacting? Depression swamped her as she walked up the path to the front door. It seemed that every time their relationship took a step forward, it was followed by two steps back.

Dorcas was in the kitchen, making coffee. She looked up as Philippa came in. 'No need to tell me. I heard voices and looked out. I can guess what happened.' She shook her head impatiently. 'Just what *are* you playing at, Pippa?'

Philippa took off her coat and sank wearily into a chair. 'I don't know. I just don't understand myself half the time. Brent asked me out this evening and I told him I was having dinner with an old friend who was in town for a few hours.'

Dorcas frowned. 'Well, that wasn't so far from the truth.'

'But he'd asked me earlier if Peter was the man I was engaged to. He knew all about him.'

Dorcas nodded. 'I see – so you didn't want him to know you were seeing Peter in case he thought you might be getting together again?'

'I – suppose so. I didn't really stop to analyse my feelings.' Philippa shook her head. 'Now I've made the whole thing look even more suspicious. Oh, *damn!*' She looked imploringly at her friend. 'It seems I just can't handle relationships any more, Dorcas.

I might as well give up! I think the best thing I can do is to look for another job.' She glanced at Dorcas. 'Anyway, I've been meaning to talk to you – when you and John get married, Simon and I are going to have to look for somewhere else to live, aren't we?'

Dorcas laughed. 'Good heavens! That won't be for months yet. Anything could happen in that time. Anyway, you look all in. This is neither the time nor the place to be having in-depth discussions about the future.' She smiled. 'Long before we come to that we shall have Christmas upon us. Have you given a thought to that yet?'

Philippa shook her head. At that moment the mere thought of it dismayed and exhausted her. 'No, I haven't,' she admitted.

'Well, I know someone who has,' Dorcas told her. 'When I went up to tuck Simon in tonight he was telling me all the things he was hoping to find in his stocking!'

During the rest of that week at the Health Centre Philippa hardly saw Brent. They were busy; the 'flu season seemed to have started in earnest and there was also an outbreak of measles cases. Fortunately Simon had already had it, for which Philippa was grateful. She seemed to have had more than her share of problems lately without that. On the Friday morning Gladys looked in to tell her she was going to the hospital for her appointment with the consultant on Monday afternoon. She seemed nervous.

'What kind of specialist is Mr Frobisher?' she asked anxiously.

'He's a general surgeon,' Philippa told her. 'He does all kinds of jobs. I hear he's a very brilliant man.'

'Oh – he's not a…' Gladys bit her lip. 'Not a…'

'Cancer specialist?' Philippa supplied. 'No, he isn't.' She smiled reassuringly at the cleaner. 'Try not to worry about it too much,' she said kindly. 'Look, is there anyone who'll go along to the hospital with you?'

'Oh no!' Gladys shook her head. 'No one knows except Doctor Charlesworth and you – and that's the way I want it. No, whatever I have to face, I'll face alone for as long as I can, anyway.'

Philippa squeezed her arm. 'This time next week it'll be all over. I'll tell you what – I'll bring a bottle of sherry and we'll have a glass on Monday evening, to celebrate. How about that?'

The cleaner gave her an anxious little smile. 'And if we don't have anything to celebrate?'

'We'll have a drink anyway. Now that's a date – right?'

After the morning rush Philippa decided to skip lunch and catch up with some of her paperwork. The Health Centre seemed blissfully quiet as she bent her head over her work; just the occasional ringing of the telephone in Reception and the muted tapping of Jenny's typewriter. Presently the typing stopped and she vaguely registered an exchange of voices in the distance. A patient must have come in to make an appointment. But a moment later her door opened and Jenny looked in.

'There's someone to see you,' she said.

Philippa frowned. 'I'm rather busy at the moment, Jenny. Is it urgent?' The person masked by the receptionist as she stood in the doorway stepped forward and Philippa saw to her surprise that it was Emma Francis. 'Oh...' She nodded to Jenny. 'It's all right, Jenny – thanks.' She indicated the chair opposite her desk. 'Please – come in and have a seat. What can I do for you?'

'I must confess that I was hoping to catch Brent,' the other girl said.

'I see.' Philippa looked at her watch. 'Well, I'm afraid he's out on his rounds at the moment. He won't be back for some time.

But if I can help…'

Emma looked uncertain. 'I don't know. I have to talk to someone. Perhaps…' She took a deep breath. 'It's Mrs Charlesworth,' she explained. 'I'm really worried about her.'

'Why, is she ill?' Philippa asked.

'I believe so, yes. I've suspected it ever since I first went to work for her, but she insisted she was all right.'

'And now something has confirmed it for you?' Philippa supplied.

The other girl nodded. 'This morning she had this – this kind of *turn*. It wasn't the first time, but this one was worse than the others. I begged her to go home, but she wouldn't. I've been trying to get her to see a doctor for days too, but she simply wouldn't hear of it.'

'Who is her doctor?' asked Philippa.

'Doctor Martin. I even rang him this morning, but Mrs Charlesworth wouldn't keep the appointment I made for her. She said it was just a sore throat and that she'd be fine if I just stopped fussing and left her alone.'

'I don't really see that I can do anything,' Philippa said doubtfully. 'After all, I've never even met her.'

Emma nodded. 'I know, but in a way that

might be an advantage. Do you think you could possibly come with me to see her?' When Philippa hesitated she went on: 'You *are* a nurse, and Miss Stone says Brent is always saying how good you are.'

'I'm not qualified to make a diagnosis, though,' Philippa warned. 'I could only give an opinion. I can't help feeling that she should be persuaded to see a doctor.'

'I know – but even if you could just do *that* it would help.' Emma shook her head. 'I'm at my wits' end. I just don't know what to do!'

Philippa looked at the girl's worried face and relented a little. 'Well, all right. I'll see what I can do, but I can't promise anything.'

Emma sprang up. 'Oh, that's wonderful! Can you come now?'

Philippa was taken aback. 'Now? You mean *right* now?'

'I wouldn't ask, but I really am worried about her.'

Philippa sighed and stood up, reaching for her coat. 'Right, I'm on my lunch hour anyway. Let's go.'

In the car, Emma filled her in with a history of Jane Charlesworth's symptoms:

'She's lost an awful lot of weight lately and she has this terrible thirst – always sending me out for cups of tea and coffee.'

Philippa asked: 'Is she on any kind of medication – insulin, for instance; have you ever seen her giving herself an injection?'

'No, I told you, she's got this thing about doctors,' Emma repeated. 'I don't think she's seen one for years.'

Jane Charlesworth's office was situated in a large block in the city centre, and Philippa stood silently beside Emma in the lift as they went up to the tenth floor. Emma glanced hesitantly at Philippa, then suddenly she said: 'I owe you an apology!'

Philippa looked at her in surprise. 'You do?'

'Yes.' Emma took a deep breath. 'I said something about you that turned out to be untrue. I thought – took it for granted that the little boy I saw you with at the school was yours, and it slipped out in conversation when Daddy and I were having dinner at the Frazers'.' She took a deep breath. 'If it's any consolation, I made a complete fool of myself and got into everyone's bad books, including Brent's.'

Philippa shrugged. 'I suppose it was a natural conclusion to come to. No harm done.'

Emma took a deep breath, obviously

relieved at having cleared the matter up. She glanced at Philippa. 'He thinks an awful lot of you, you know. I suppose I was jealous – but…' Philippa had no time to hear the rest of her sentence, at that moment the lift stopped and she followed Emma along the corridor.

The moment they entered the office Philippa could see that Emma hadn't been exaggerating. Jane Charlesworth was lying slumped over her desk. She muttered incoherently as they came in. Philippa lost no time. The moment she raised the woman's head she caught the characteristic odour of apples on her breath. Emma, standing close by, sniffed.

'I've smelt that before,' she said. 'Like nail varnish. What does it mean?'

'Get me some sugar – quick!' Philippa commanded. 'Dissolve a large spoonful in a glass of warm water, but make it quick. She'll go into a coma if she doesn't get it. Then ring for an ambulance. Tell them it's urgent!'

At the hospital Philippa waited with Emma while Jane Charlesworth was whisked up to the ward. Presently a nurse came to tell them that she was conscious and comfortable and that they could see her if they wished. Philippa looked at Emma doubtfully.

'I'd better go now,' she said. 'Anyway, Mrs Charlesworth won't want to see me. She doesn't even know me.'

But Emma took her arm and held it tightly. 'She most certainly *will* want to see you. After all, she has a lot to thank you for. I wouldn't have had a clue what to do. Please come up with me.'

So Philippa followed her up to the ward where Jane Charlesworth lay, her face pale against the pillows and a saline drip in her arm. She smiled at the two girls.

'I owe thanks to you both,' she said. 'They tell me I might have been in serious trouble if I hadn't arrived when I did. The doctor has been telling me off for not taking proper care of myself.' She looked at Philippa. 'We haven't met before, Nurse James, though I have heard about you through my sister. Please accept my sincere thanks for what you did this afternoon.'

'I'm just glad Emma brought me to you in time,' said Philippa. She was looking at the woman in the bed, thinking how like his mother Brent was – the same blue-green eyes and corn-coloured hair. Their eyes met and Jane smiled. 'I'm glad we've met at last, though I could have wished for happier circumstances.' She looked at Emma. 'Don't wait any longer, dear. I shall be perfectly all right now. I was expecting a call at the office and I'd like someone to be there to take it.'

Emma took the hint, rising and holding out her hand to Philippa. 'Goodbye, then. And thanks again.' She smiled at her employer. 'I'll come and see you again this evening.'

When she had gone Philippa made to move, but Jane reached out to prevent her. 'Don't go yet, my dear. I sent Emma away because I wanted to have a word with you. Brent and I don't see much of each other, as you probably know, but I keep in touch with what he's doing through my sister.' She turned to look at Philippa thoughtfully 'I dare say he's told you about me – the mother who neglected him.' She sighed. 'I'd like you to understand a little of what it was like. When my husband died I took the firm over because it was our livelihood. I wanted it to be alive and flourishing for Brent when he grew up; after all, that was what his father had worked for all those years. It was hard at first – very hard, but later I admit that it took hold of me. I began to enjoy it, to be totally involved. I don't know quite how it happened, but before I knew it I'd lost my son – the one person I'd done it all for. He went his own way and didn't even want the one thing I'd sacrificed everything to build for him. In fact he resented it bitterly.' She turned to smile at Philippa. 'Can you understand how that made me feel?'

Philippa nodded. 'Yes, I think so,' she said quietly.

'Angela tells me that you are bringing up a little boy – your brother's child,' Jane went on. 'Take a tip from me. Don't make too many sacrifices for him. Love him and enjoy his childhood all you can, but remember that in the end he has to be a person in his own right – and that you have a life too.'

Philippa moistened her dry lips. 'I'll remember – but why...'

'Why am I saying all this to you?' Jane supplied. 'Let's just say that I believe in repaying a kindness.' She sighed. 'It goes without saying that I'd rather you didn't mention this to – to...' Her eyelids drooped with fatigue, and Philippa rose to her feet.

'You must rest now, Mrs Charlesworth,' she said. 'I'm sure you'll be better soon. I'm glad I was able to help, and if you need me at any time...' She covered the limp white

hand that rested on the sheet. 'Thank you –
for what you've just told me.'

At the entrance to the ward she stopped to
look back at the sick woman. Her eyes were
closed and she looked ill and exhausted.
How could two people who were so close
have misunderstood each other so tragically
over the years? she wondered. She made up
her mind there and then that no such misunderstanding would spoil her relationship
with Simon.

It was only as she was getting into her car
that she caught sight of the clock above the
hospital entrance. Afternoon surgery would
have begun half an hour ago! They would be
wondering what had happened to her. She
started the car and headed for the Health
Centre as fast as she could.

There was a long queue of patients outside
her door when she arrived, and it was after
four by the time she had attended to the last
of them. Jenny brought her a cup of tea after
she had ushered the last patient out, but she
had barely had time to put it down on the
desk when Brent strode into the room, his
eyes flashing angrily.

'I expected you to offer some explanation
when you finally deigned to put in an
appearance this afternoon!' he snapped.

Jenny scuttled from the room, closing the door tactfully behind her. When he got no reply Brent moved closer, to tower over Philippa as she sat at her desk. 'What was it, then – an extended lunch with your ex-fiancé?'

She looked up at him. 'As it happens, no.' She stood up and began to put on her coat. 'As it happens I was at the hospital. I was just coming to speak to you, as a matter of fact.'

He looked taken aback. 'The hospital – Simon again?'

She turned to face him. 'No, Brent, not Simon. Your mother. I'm afraid she's been developing diabetes for some time, and this afternoon she collapsed. Emma came here looking for you, but I was the only one here at the time. We managed to get your mother to the hospital before she went into a coma, luckily.' She walked to the door, turning to him, her hand on the handle. 'I think you should go and see her, Brent. She needs you. I think the two of you should talk.'

He glared at her, suddenly stung into life. 'I think you can safely leave decisions of that kind to me, Philippa,' he snapped. 'Thank you for letting me know, but maybe you'd have done better minding your own business! Jenny could have contacted me, you know, even if I was out at the time.'

Wounded to the core, Philippa opened the door and let herself out, making her way out of the building. She didn't see Jenny's curious glance as she passed Reception, so blinded was she by tears. Once inside her car, she surrendered to them, telling herself that he wasn't worth her tears. Mrs Charlesworth deserved them far more. It was lucky that she had found out what Brent was really like before it was too late! But deep inside she knew it *was* too late. Nothing could stop her loving him now – nothing could insulate her from his devastating power to hurt her.

At home she put on a brave face for Simon's sake, but when she came downstairs after tucking him up for the night Dorcas tackled her.

'All right – *give!*'

Philippa looked at her, bravely attempting to pretend she didn't understand, but she didn't have a chance against the other girl's perceptive probing.

'It's obvious that you haven't cleared up the misunderstanding over Peter,' Dorcas went on. 'And by the look of you it's worse than I thought. So why not tell me all about it and we'll see if we can untangle the mess together?'

Philippa sank on to the settee with a sigh. 'You're right, we haven't cleared anything up. Brent quite clearly isn't prepared to listen to anything I have to say. He isn't interested. And anyway, he has something else to think about now...' She went on to recount to Dorcas the events of the afternoon and Brent's cool acceptance of the news of his mother's illness. 'He's almost like two people,' she finished. 'On Saturday he was so gentle with Simon and – and with me. Today, when I told him about his mother, he told me to – to mind my own business.' She looked at Dorcas, her eyes dark with pain. 'I've decided, Dorcas,' she said. 'I'm going to have to move again. It's been lovely, living here with you. Simon and I have been so happy, but it just isn't on any more – for all kinds of reasons.'

'Look, if you're thinking that because John and I are going to be married...' Dorcas stopped speaking as Philippa got to her feet.

'That's only part of it,' she said. 'One of the many things that tells me it's time to move on.' Dorcas was speechless for once and Philippa smiled what she hoped was a reassuring smile. 'I'll always be grateful to you for all you've done for Simon and me,' she said sincerely. 'But as soon as Christmas is behind us I'm going to look for another job – as far away from Castlebridge as I can get.'

Late on Monday afternoon Gladys arrived at the Health Centre and came looking for Philippa, her face beaming.

'It was just as you said!' she said, bubbling over with relief. 'Mr Frobisher said it was a cyst. He drained off the fluid and told me he was ninety-nine per cent it was harmless. It didn't hurt a bit! I have to go back in three weeks just to check, but he says I'm not to worry any more. Isn't it great?'

Philippa shared her relief, pouring her the glass of sherry she had promised. Gladys sat down to drink it, looking relaxed for the first time in weeks. 'By the way,' she said chattily as she sipped the drink, 'while I was at the hospital I slipped up to see Mrs Charlesworth. Jenny told me she'd been taken poorly.' Noticing Philippa's enquiring look, she added, 'Oh, I used to clean for her before she moved out of town. I expect you've heard she's got diabetes? Such a shame, poor love.' She leaned forward. 'It's an ill wind, though. Guess what – she told me that Doctor is taking her away for a holiday when she comes out in a few days' time – to help her recover. They haven't been friendly for a long time, you know. I was so pleased for her. She's a nice lady.' She sighed. 'Funny how things work out, isn't it?'

Philippa sighed reflectively. Funny wasn't quite the word she would have chosen.

Mrs Charlesworth came out of hospital the following week, and true to Gladys's word, Brent let it be known that he was taking two weeks off. Jenny confirmed that what Gladys had said was true; he was taking his mother away to convalesce. Philippa was stung. He hadn't come to tell her personally. He hadn't spoken to her since the afternoon his mother was taken ill and he left a few days later without seeing her again.

Resigned to the fact that she must leave Castlebridge, Philippa combed the nursing journals for another job. It wasn't going to be any easier than it had been the first time, and she kept putting off the task of telling Simon that they must uproot themselves once more. At last, on Dorcas's advice, she shelved the idea and started on her Christmas preparations. Simon was getting so excited; she must not allow her depression to transmit itself to him too.

She and Dorcas wrote Christmas cards, struggled round the crowded shops and took it in turns to bake batches of mince pies and sausage rolls – a large Christmas cake, plum puddings. The house was full of the spicy aromas and Simon, his excitement barely contained, 'helped', at every opportunity, stirring the luscious mixtures and licking the bowls clean.

Philippa went to the school concert and she and Simon attended the play that Dorcas had produced. They sat with John, on whose face the pride shone quite unashamedly, and Philippa felt her heart twist with pain. This Christmas might have been so happy, so different – if only…

On the Sunday before Christmas they trimmed the tree after Simon had gone to bed. Dorcas was talking about the arrangements they had made. John was to join them on Christmas Day and on Boxing Day he was taking Dorcas to his parents.

'Are you sure you and Simon will be all right on your own?' Dorcas asked for the hundredth time as she fixed the fairy to the top of the tree.

'If I've told you once I've told you a dozen

times,' Philippa told her with a sigh, 'we'll be fine. Simon will have all his new toys to play with and by then I'll be glad to put my feet up.'

But Dorcas looked unconvinced. 'I wish you'd change your mind about leaving, Pippa,' she said, sitting back on her heels. 'When Brent gets back...'

'When Brent gets back life will be doubly impossible,' Philippa told her firmly.

'But Simon is happy here. Think what it will do to him,' protested Dorcas. 'He was asking me the other day when Brent was coming back and if he'd be around at Christmas.'

Philippa sighed. 'That alone should tell you why I can't stay. I don't only have myself to think of, do I?'

At the Health Centre the winter rush tailed off, almost as though people were putting off their ailments until after the holiday. It was late on the afternoon of Christmas Eve that the telephone rang on Philippa's desk just as she was leaving for home. She stared at it; another second and she would have been gone. Should she let it remain unanswered? But even as the thought was passing through her mind she was reaching out her hand for the receiver.

'Hello, Castlebridge Health Centre. Nurse James speaking.'

'Philippa?'

'Yes.' She didn't recognise the voice and wondered who could be calling who knew her Christian name.

'It's Jane Charlesworth here.'

'Oh! How are you?'

'Much better, thank you. Learning to cope with my wretched diabetes now, thank goodness. Brent has been so wonderful – such a help.'

'I'm glad. Did you have a nice holiday?'

'Lovely! I'm calling to ask what you're doing over Christmas, Philippa.'

She was taken aback. 'Oh – well, not a lot really. Children are happy just to be at home with their presents, aren't they?'

'If you've nothing arranged would you like to come for tea on Boxing Day?' asked Jane. 'And bring your little nephew too, of course. It's so long since I entertained a small boy at Christmas – I'd love it. I'd like to have the chance to thank you properly for what you did too. Do say you'll come.'

Philippa felt she could hardly refuse. 'Well, that sounds lovely,' she said. 'I'm sure we'd both enjoy it very much. Thank you.'

'Wonderful – around two, shall we say?

See you then.' She gave Philippa the address and directions for finding her house, then said goodbye and rang off.

Christmas Day passed in a flurry of present-opening, eating and drinking, and the following morning Dorcas was up bright and early to be ready for John when he arrived to drive her over to his parents' house. Philippa and Simon ate a lunch of cold turkey, then got ready to drive over to Long Norton, the village where Jane Charlesworth lived.

The moment Simon saw the house he exclaimed with delight: 'Oh look, Pippa, it's just like the Gingerbread House!' He was right. Rook's Cottage was long and low with a thatched roof and pretty latticed windows. Jane Charlesworth came out to meet them, tall and slim and a hundred per cent better than the last time Philippa had seen her. Simon took to her at once and was soon chatting away to her, telling her all about his Christmas presents. Jane laughed, bending to take both his hands.

'Simon, the man next door has some baby rabbits. Before you take off your coat, would you like to come and see them?'

'Oh, yes, *please!*'

She straightened up and looked at

Philippa. 'Take off your coat and go into the sitting room,' she invited. 'There's a nice log fire in there. We shan't be long.'

Thinking vaguely that it was rather strange, carting Simon off the moment they arrived, Philippa took off her coat and hung it in the hall, then pushed open the door Jane had indicated – then she stopped dead in her tracks. There was a blazing log fire, as Jane had said – but, standing in front of it, his eyes on the door, stood Brent. He looked tanned and handsome after his holiday and the sight of him took her breath away.

'Oh!'

The corners of his mouth twitched. 'Is that all you have to say?'

'I – er – how are you, Brent?' she asked, feeling foolish. 'Did you – have a good holiday?'

'Not really,' he told her. 'I couldn't stop thinking what an ungrateful swine I'd been – couldn't stop wanting to come back and see you – to apologise.'

'There was no need,' she said awkwardly, glancing behind her. 'Your mother and Simon have gone next door. I wonder…'

He crossed the room and closed the door firmly. 'They'll be quite a long time,' he told her. 'It was all arranged. I warned her this could take quite some time and I've a feeling I was right.' He faced her. 'Philippa, I have to know. Are you – do you feel anything for me at all – apart from anger at the way I've behaved, I mean?'

She stared at him, feeling as though someone had knocked all the breath from her body. 'I...' But Brent didn't wait to hear any more. Grasping her by the shoulders, he pulled her towards him and kissed her long and hard. As their lips parted he sighed and drew her closer, resting his chin on the top of her head.

'If you only knew how much I've ached to do that over the past weeks,' he told her softly. 'If you knew how insanely jealous I was of Peter Gilbert! You've aroused emotions in me I never knew myself capable of, Pippa. I only hope you're prepared to take the consequences.'

She looked up at him, her heart racing with happiness. 'Oh, Brent – if you'd just *said!* You left without even saying goodbye – I thought...'

He shook his head. 'I couldn't bear to say goodbye, because I thought it might be final.' He looked down at her. 'We've both done far too much *thinking* in the past. From now on it's going to be cards on the table – right?' She nodded and he kissed her softly. 'I love you, Pippa. I believe I have since that first day, at your interview, when I tried so hard to tie you up in knots. Maybe I had some kind of premonition of what was about to happen to me!' He laughed. 'You see, you're teaching me so much about myself.' His eyes were suddenly serious as he asked quietly: 'Well, what do you say? Do you think you could bear the thought of spending a lifetime with me – marrying me?'

Philippa took a deep, shuddering breath. 'Of course I can. I love you too, Brent,' she whispered. 'It's something I've been struggling to come to terms with for ages. But do you realise what you'd be taking on?'

'Simon?' He shook his head. 'Simon is part of it all,' he told her. 'He made me see you for what you are.' His eyes twinkled. 'Anyway, I hope it won't be long before he's mingling with the crowd!'

Her eyes opened wide. 'If you mean what I *think* you mean…!'

He pulled her back into his arms and held her tightly. 'From now on I mean *everything* I say. We have a lot of lost time to make up. I want you – and Simon and *our* children – all of them! That's the deal, Pippa James.

Take it or leave it!' He looked down into her eyes.

'I'll take it,' she told him happily.

The publishers hope that this book has given you enjoyable reading. Large Print Books are especially designed to be as easy to see and hold as possible. If you wish a complete list of our books please ask at your local library or write directly to:

Dales Large Print Books
Magna House, Long Preston,
Skipton, North Yorkshire.
BD23 4ND

This Large Print Book, for people *Joe*
who cannot read normal print,
is published under the auspices of

THE ULVERSCROFT FOUNDATION

... we hope you have enjoyed this book.
Please think for a moment about those
who have worse eyesight than you ...
and are unable to even read or enjoy
Large Print without great difficulty.

You can help them by sending a
donation, large or small, to:

**The Ulverscroft Foundation,
1, The Green, Bradgate Road,
Anstey, Leicestershire, LE7 7FU,
England.**
or request a copy of our brochure for
more details.

The Foundation will use all donations
to assist those people who are visually
impaired and need special attention
with medical research, diagnosis
and treatment.

Thank you very much for your help.